JINA S. BAZZAR

IMPERIAL STARDUST

THE MACLEE CHRONICLES BOOK 2

Copyright (C) 2024 Jina S. Bazzar.

This book is a work of fiction. Names, characters, places, and incidents are the product of the author's imagination or are used fictitiously. Any resemblance to actual events, locales, or persons, living or dead, is purely coincidental.

All rights reserved. No part of this book may be reproduced or transmitted in any form or by any means, electronic or mechanical, including photocopying, recording, or by any information storage and retrieval system, without the author's permission.

Cover design by MiblArt.

Imperial Stardust

Chapter 1

I was on the bridge of the *Splendor*, the port view screen showcasing a stunning view of Krozalia, when a piercing screech broke the calm of the moment. I was jolted from my thoughts of a certain Kroz and would have tumbled from the pilot's chair if I hadn't been strapped in.

"Flip me sideways and toggle my control, you bitches!"

"Mac!" I shrieked, jerking in my seat.

"What?" Sullivan asked from the co-pilot's chair, looking around in alarm. "Who the hell is Mac?"

The moment I'd announced we were entering gravity, Sullivan had come—alone—claiming Ravi wanted to stand guard over the princess. Something about re-entry making her sick, but I hadn't paid attention past "not coming".

I had a feeling the Krozalian head guard needed some distance to regain the balance he'd lost after that earth-shattering kiss. It gave me some warm fuzzies that I wasn't sure were entirely good.

"I, um, my cat," I stuttered, fumbling for a lie. "I just remembered I forgot to leave food out for my cat."

Sullivan was eyeing me as if I had sprouted horns, an extra head, or maybe a wart. "You have a cat?" he asked slowly, carefully, as if the words didn't want to come out of his mouth.

"If you did, that unfortunate baby would be dead by now," Mac said in my ear. "Poor thing."

"I did, I mean, I do."

"On Cyrus Station?"

"No, at home."

"And home is?"

I glared at him. "Nice try."

Sullivan shrugged. "Doesn't hurt to ask."

"It would when your superiors demand to know and you find yourself obliged to spill."

Sullivan winced. "Fair enough. Keep your address to yourself. I'm sure Admiral Fulk won't need to compel me or anyone else if he wants to know."

Not true. My address wasn't in my name—it was in Baltsar's. And it was just a place I bunked in whenever I was in the station and wanted something more substantial than the *Splendor* around me. But I had no doubt Admiral Fulk would put his best on the task of tracking my address if he decided he wanted the knowledge.

"Is that Krozalia?" Mac asked in my ear. "Damn, woman. I leave you for…six days!" he screeched again, the piercing sound making my eyes water. I gritted my teeth as Mac freaked out. "Why the hell was I off for six whole days? Why didn't you reboot me?"

"I did. Several times," I said sub-vocally. "Nothing worked."

"You called for him when you were unconscious," Sullivan remarked, eyes downcast as he fiddled with his console. "Is Mac a lover or something?"

Mac chortled in my ear.

I cast a sideways glance at Sullivan. "I don't have a lover," I told him.

Sullivan's eyebrows went up, but he still didn't look at me.

Hooded umber eyes flashed in my mind. The sensation of Ravi's mouth on mine, his hands roaming my body—something inside me tightened and made me blush. "Mac is my pet," I reiterated.

"I should take offense to that," Mac grumbled.

"What about you and the Kroz?" Sullivan asked next.

I fumbled and swiveled to face him fully. Had Ravi told him about the kiss? I doubted that. Besides, a kiss might have been a prelude to something, but we were far from lovers.

"What do you mean?"

Sullivan tapped aimlessly on his screen as if it was the most fascinating thing he'd ever done.

"Sunny?"

He dropped his hand and turned piercing blue eyes on me. "I saw you two lip-locked, so please, don't act stupid."

"Ooh, which one?" Mac asked.

"I'm not sure what you want me to say," I began, feeling awkward. "I don't see how me kissing Ravi is any of your business."

"But it's mine," Mac interjected. "Tell me. Who jumped whom?"

Sullivan grimaced. "I didn't mean it like that. It's just," he met my eyes, and the misery in them took me aback. "You were always discreet with your love life. I don't think I've ever seen you hanging out with a lover, much less kissing someone in the open."

My face heated. "I'm just a private person."

Sullivan sighed. "I know that. But one regret is that I never got to ask you out. After the Genesis Mission, I realized that even if I'd known my chances were slim, I failed for never trying. I didn't know your preferences, and I didn't know which way you leaned, but it wasn't an excuse. I'd always been afraid to cross the line you erected to keep people out."

"I didn't know," I admitted softly. I'd never seen Sullivan as anything but a fellow team member, a soldier of the Confederacy. He'd never been anything more, never a potential, regardless of the fact that he'd always attracted women whenever we were on leave. He was good looking; I knew that because I had two functioning eyes, but he was just...Sullivan, my squad mate and friend.

"Sunny," I began, completely out of words.

"Please," he interrupted. "I don't want your sympathy or pity. Don't look at me like that."

I gave a jerky nod and clasped and unclasped my fingers.

"I'm sorry."

Sullivan raked a hand through his hair and shook his head. "I'm not sure why I said all this. It's just, I spent ten years regretting never saying anything. I see now I shouldn't have." He gave a rueful shrug. "I learned that it's better to regret doing something than regret never doing it. This way, I don't have to also wonder about the outcome."

"I'm sorry," I said again.

"Don't be." He nodded at the Krozalian planet. "How long do you think we'll be there for?"

I glanced back at the blue and green planet, grateful for the topic change. "I don't know."

"Have you ever been there before?"

"No. You?"

"No," he replied. "I've never left Confederacy Space, save for small excursions to the edge of Sector 7 and 9."

The rest of the journey went by in silence, interrupted by Mac's occasional comment. We landed on a private field not so far from the castle. On three sides, large cliffs jutted above turbulent waters, dense with rocks and white with froth. On foot, there was only one way in and out, and that way was through the castle.

I landed the *Splendor* on the exact coordinates Ravi had given Sullivan. The royal escorts kept pace with us, landing when we did, surrounding the *Splendor*.

"That doesn't look so friendly," Sullivan said, bringing the 360-view outside to the port view screen.

We were in the middle of the field, and all escorts had their bows pointing toward the *Splendor*.

"They're all equidistant from each other, using us as the center," Mac observed. "I wonder how long that formation took them to perfect."

"Is there a significance to it?" I asked sub-vocally.

"Safety and prestige, I'm guessing. Usually, the ship in the middle is a diplomatic one."

That made sense, considering the princess and Head of

the Royal Guard were both aboard the ship.

I gave everyone the signal to disembark while I locked everything down and shut off the engines, leaving the console on standby so Mac wasn't locked out of the ship. His main matrix was embedded in my right wrist, but there was a smaller chip that Baltsar had put into the *Splendor*. It meant that Mac didn't always need to see out my right eye to keep tabs on our surroundings. He also had admin access to the ship's network system, which he used to hack into other networks. It was the reason we tapped Leo for information—although Mac was an expert at cracking secure systems, any mistakes would lead others straight to the *Splendor*.

When there was nothing left to do, I packed a small duffle and made my way to the ramp, my anxiety high.

The glare of the sun, the humidity, and the salty air invoked memories of my youth, playing by the shore of my parents' summer cottage. But then my steps took me into view of the outside world and the illusion of warmth and safety shattered. Kroz in uniform were everywhere, ten, fifteen, more than twenty. All wore the same dark uniform with no insignia. None that I could see from where I stood, but I didn't need to. I knew what it was.

Kroz armor.

I had only seen it once in person during a military parade in my early days at the academy when a Kroz warrior had attended a CTF peace attempt with the Cradox—the race the humans had been fighting on and off for so long.

I'd also watched them in action in plenty of holographic vids. The elite of the Kroz elite. Warriors who were dispatched for the worst and most dangerous cases.

Like a case involving a hypermorph.

My mouth went dry and my heart beat like a mad drum in my throat. I wiped my suddenly sweaty palms on the legs of my pants. Their presence didn't mean they were here for me— Dolenta, the princess and only heir to the Krozalian throne, was important enough to warrant such a show of force.

Ravi stood apart with six other Kroz, one of whom was a redheaded woman. If I had to guess, I'd say they were the captains of the escort ships.

Dolenta stood a few steps behind him, clearly separate, but still within his reach. They were all listening to what Ravi was saying, faces grim as he no doubt filled them in on Thern's betrayal. *Would he tell them about me too?*

"Can you hear what they're saying?" I asked Mac.

"Hold a second," Mac said. "No. It's all gibberish. I think it's some sort of code between them. That, or the translator I downloaded has malfunctioned."

Prickling on the side of my head had me looking around at the other Kroz scattered about. Their uniform gleamed under the sun like water, beautiful despite the simplicity. No one had their helmets on, making it easier for me to find the ones staring at me.

There were two.

One was bald with the tattoo of the Tanue covering his entire scalp, and the other was a Kroz with long sandy hair that looked casually tousled. He winked and smiled at me when our eyes met. I looked away. They weren't doing anything but standing there, clearly bored and waiting for orders.

Ahead of me and to the side, arms clasped behind their backs, standing at parade rest were Sullivan, Lorenzo, and Cassandra. I wondered if I was supposed to be standing with them. Cassandra caught me looking and motioned me over, deciding for me.

While I couldn't see Ravi's face from this angle, and knew for a fact that the Kroz didn't have eyes in the backs of their heads, the moment I descended the ramp, he gave a nod to the group and turned to face me. The woman, I noted, turned with him. She wore the black uniform like everyone else, but she made it look good, the material hugging her curves and bringing out her creamy complexion. Jealousy reared its head so fast that I missed my next step and stumbled, almost face-planting. Lorenzo's snickering followed and cut out abruptly. My face heated with embarrassment.

"Your heart rate just amped up to one-hundred-and-twelve," Mac observed. "What happened? I didn't see anything."

"Why? What are you doing?"

"I asked first."

While Mac could use my right eye as his personal camera to see what I saw, he didn't have access to my emotions and my thoughts. For him, I had tripped over my own feet and nothing more.

"Nothing." I shoved all the confusing emotions into the back of my mind. Later, when I was alone, I'd examine my reactions and my feelings. Right now, there were too many eyes on me—including Ravi's.

"Tell me what you are up to," I demanded. While he didn't devote all his time experiencing the world through my eye, it was rare for him to miss much of what happened around me. Unless...

"Trying to crack the Gamat Com server," He replied. "I figured it was best to make up for lost time since we don't know how long we'll be here."

My nerves quivered at the thought. We were already in hot waters without adding the breach of government companies to the list of transgressions. "Don't," I said as I descended the rest of the ramp to meet Ravi.

"I'm sorry, did you just tell me no? It must be a joke—a poor one, I should add," Mac said.

"Not a joke, though I wish it was. Process the feed from the *Splendor* for the past six days and then we'll talk about it."

It took Ravi forever to close the gap between us, but it was really only twenty or so meters. The woman paused by Cassandra and extended a hand, smiling as she said something that made her laugh out loud.

"Leann," Ravi said and reluctantly, I met his eyes.

He took another step forward, invading my personal space, then another. He leaned close to my ear, his warm breath making me shiver. "I need you to take the ship to the port so I can retrieve Thern." He brushed his lips over my cheek, then pressed them against my mouth. "Zafra will come with you to show the way," he murmured, sending tingling pricks all over my body. He nipped my bottom lip; then, as if the temptation was too much to resist, closed his mouth over mine. My lips parted in invitation and my hands clutched fistfuls of his tunic. His tongue slid in and stroked mine. He tasted even better than the first time: of dark promises and long nights and exotic wishes.

"I don't understand the allure of exchanging spit," Mac said with disgust. "I'll go watch that feed now and leave you to finish this repulsive ritual."

It took me several seconds to focus after Ravi broke the kiss. "Okay?"

"Huh?"

Ravi leaned back a few inches, eyes lacking any of the hunger I'd seen on the bridge. "Thern. I need to retrieve him from the ship without an audience."

The words felt like a well-placed slap: it made my face burn. That had been an act for those watching, Kroz and CTF alike. Mortification had my embarrassment igniting like a supernova. My arms dropped to my sides. Before I could put some distance between us, Ravi's mask slipped, replaced by burning need. He leaned close again and I stopped him with a hand to his chest. He didn't try to kiss me, touching his forehead to mine and sighing instead. "What am I going to do with you?"

I cleared my throat. "Um, nothing?"

He chuckled, eyes crinkling at the corners. His gaze scanned mine from millimeters away, and for a moment there, I wondered if he could see the difference between my right and left eye.

"I wish we were alone," Ravi breathed, either because he was as private a person as I was, or because he'd picked up on my unease. He straightened and took a large step back. "Now. Can you do this?"

I swallowed and tried a smile I hoped didn't look as

shaky as it felt. "Of course."

"Zafra will accompany you and show you the way." He took another step back.

I wasn't sure if he gave a signal or what, but the tall redhead was suddenly beside him, studying me with curious, metallic-green eyes.

"Show Captain Lee her accommodations once you're done," he said to the Kroz woman in Universal. Without waiting for a reply, he turned and began walking away, calling over his shoulder, "I'll escort the princess to the emperor. Please show the captain to the spaceport where she can store her ship for the duration of her stay."

Since he'd already said that to me, I figured the repetition was for the benefit of everyone else.

Ravi motioned to one of the nearby Kroz. "Syam, please show Commodore Lorenzo and his companions to the guest wing and arrange for their comfort."

Syam inclined his head with a "sir" and stepped close to Lorenzo.

"I'm Zafra," the redhead said to me, extending a hand.

I took it automatically and shook. "Leann." Her hand was firm, calloused, and cool.

"Shall we?" she asked, motioning to the ship behind me.

"Yes," I said, and with a last look to where Syam was escorting the others away, I headed back aboard the *Splendor*.

Chapter 2

I dropped into the pilot's seat and started the engine, my hands not as steady as I'd have liked them to be.

"May I?" Zafra asked.

I glanced up and found her beside the co-pilot's chair, waiting for my permission to sit.

My opinion of her went up a notch. "Yes. Go ahead."

She slid into the seat with liquid grace, and it dawned on me that she was probably as dangerous as Ravi. Not only was she captain of her ship, but she was captain of a royal guard ship.

Zafra scanned the control panel with curiosity, maybe even a bit of intrigue, but kept her hands folded on her lap, not touching anything.

"It's rude to stare, you know?" Mac said in my ear.

"Where to?" I asked her.

"Not far," Zafra replied and keyed the coordinates into the screen, along with a route.

It only took us three minutes to get to the sprawling spaceship port, and it went by in total silence. I had the impression Zafra wanted to say something and kept myself braced for some possessive nonsense about Ravi, but nothing came. Maybe Kroz women didn't care about monogamous relationships. Or maybe Zafra and Ravi were simply friends. Just because I hadn't liked seeing her so close to Ravi didn't mean they were lovers or anything.

Neither are you, that little voice said in my head.

The spaceport was a large structure with massive front doors and an open roof located in the middle of an island. A large spiral tower with a polished red façade stood a few hundred meters away, closer to another cliff overlooking turquoise waters. We entered the port through the roof. I expected it to be dim and busy, but it was brightly lit and almost empty—considering its size.

"I'll escort you to your accommodations," Zafra announced when I landed the *Splendor* at the far back of the port. I wasn't sure if the location was of importance; there were plenty of empty hangars and less than a hundred ships in the entire place. We could have parked anywhere, but Zafra had directed me to this spot.

"Thank you," I said, though it wasn't like I had any other choice, seeing that I'd need a guide and transportation back.

"There's some kind of magnetic field underneath the entire back area," Mac informed me. "Could be used to lock a ship in place, I think, though I have yet to examine it closer."

"Don't," I warned.

"Pardon?" Zafra gave me an inquisitive look.

I shook my head and said nothing. I didn't think she could hear sub-vocal sounds, but I also didn't know what type of magic she possessed. For all I knew, subsonic hearing could be her passive talent.

Zafra followed me out of the ship, her stride synchronized with mine despite her legs being way longer.

We both paused outside. Me to take in the sheer enormity of the port, and Zafra...I wasn't sure. Maybe she was waiting for Ravi to come retrieve Thern. I didn't know what was keeping the Kroz traitor contained, and I wasn't stupid enough to check. For all I knew, the moment I unlocked the door, Thern could attack me. I rubbed a hand over the spot where he'd shot me with his laser gun, feeling grateful for all my enhancements. If it hadn't been for them, I'd have died countless times before this journey was over.

"This way," Zafra said, motioning to the far corner. The corner where a simple hovercraft sat. I hesitated. Were we just going to leave the *Splendor* here until Ravi finished what he was doing? How did he plan to unlock the ship to retrieve Thern? I wasn't going to give anyone clearance to waltz in and out of my ship at will. Not even him.

I bit my lower lip and contemplated calling him to clarify this part. But he was meeting with the emperor, and—call me naïve—I didn't think he would answer me.

One of the slick royal ships dropped from the roof opening then. Relieved, I released my commlink back into my pocket. But it wasn't Ravi who came for Thern. The ship landed a few meters to the right of the *Splendor* and out climbed five Kroz, all wearing the liquid black uniform, all heads and shoulders taller than me. All grim-faced.

I tensed, unsure if they were friendly or not. I cursed myself for agreeing to be isolated with people I'd never met before.

"Easy," Zafra said to me. To the Kroz, she issued a single word in Krozalian and motioned with one hand. The five Kroz stopped at once. They kept their hands open, posture relaxed, and eyed me curiously.

"This is my squad," Zafra explained and pointed at a thin Kroz so pale, I imagined he lived somewhere far from the sun. "That's Dromez, my second." Her finger moved to the Kroz beside him. "Jazzy, Tregoe, Dalman, and Evo. They're here to make sure the retrieval goes smoothly."

I recognized the blonde winker, Jazzy, and the bald Kroz, Evo, who'd been staring at me earlier.

When my silence continued, Zafra added, "If you prefer us not to board, we'll guard the ship and wait for Lord Drax to finish with the emperor."

I pursed my lips, contemplating my options. Ravi had told me when I'd awakened from the last merge with Mac that every person from the royal escort was a trusted member of his platoon. But that was before Thern had revealed himself as a traitor, and I couldn't dismiss the fact that he'd also trusted Thern implicitly. I didn't think my caution was exaggerated, but at the same time, I didn't want to prolong a situation that had already taken too much time.

"I'd rather wait for his clearance," I said gingerly.

"Very well," Zafra said without any hint of irritation. To her teammates—with the authority of a military commander—she said in Universal, "At ease."

Evo's eyes tightened with annoyance or impatience, but the rest simply spread out. Two sat on the ground where they'd previously stood, one leaned against the *Splendor's* hull to wait, and Jazzy pulled out his commlink and began playing with it.

Mac sighed. "You can't just choose the easy path, can you?"

Chapter 3

Lord Drax
I stood by the expansive windows overlooking the cliffs and blue-gray waters, waiting for the emperor to finish reassuring himself that his daughter had returned safely. It was a sign of trust and respect that he'd asked me to wait here instead of in the more formal receiving room.

Not many people had the privilege of witnessing the emperor as just a man, a father, a grieving one at that. The princess, too. She'd held on to her composure remarkably well despite being terrified. She had done better than most guards under pressure, a testament that she was stronger than the rebels believed her to be, regardless of her affinity. I had no doubt that with the right training and some creativity, the princess would be able to bring down the fiercest opponent with the flick of a finger.

The challenge was finding a mentor with similar or compatible magic to help her harness and refine her potential. While every Kroz was born with an Ashak—the gland responsible for the storage of magic—not everyone had the ability to manipulate it. Some lived their entire lives with nothing but passive magic, like the ability to predict the weather, or being able to read other people's mood. But some could control their Ashak and shape energy at will. Weather prediction became the ability to conjure rain, or strong winds, or even a tempest. Mood detection became the ability to cause unstoppable tears, fits of laughter, or induce enough terror to stop a heart. There wasn't a Kroz out there with active magic that couldn't weaponize their energy—save for Dolenta.

Imperial Stardust

Kroz with active magic were dangerous, prone to deadly accidents without severe control and discipline. They were brought early on to the Royal Academy to undergo rigorous training, where they stayed until they had mastered their Ashak. Once control had been attained, they had the choice to assume positions of power in the Krozalian government or become warriors.

Each Kroz had their own method to control their Ashak, which they learned under the guidance of a mentor with a similar affinity. I'd inherited my father's affinity and was mentored by him. Dolenta, being a dowser, had no one to teach her, and her control was adequate at best, mediocre at worst. The emperor's affinity was with blood and couldn't be more dissimilar than his daughter's. It had been always assumed that the empress would teach Dolenta, but her death had twisted that plan and left us flailing in the wind.

I watched Dolenta as she was led away by her maid, the emperor doing the same beside me. His hands flexed as if he wanted to reach out to his daughter, strangle someone, strike something, or do all three at the same time.

Emperor Rokoskiv was a powerful man, and he had the capability to do much worse if he wanted to. Sadly, this was the most emotion I'd seen him display since his mate had died. For the past three years, he'd neglected his duties, delegating whatever he could and halfheartedly doing the things he couldn't pass on to someone else.

"Tell me," the emperor demanded once the princess was out of hearing range.

I did, starting with the attack on the *Wedva-Xa*, my personal ship, and our escape in the confined evacuation pod to V-5, until Thern's subsequent capture. It was the fierce look of retribution in the emperor's eyes that made me realize that perhaps the danger to his daughter's life had completely snapped him out of the fugue he'd submerged himself into for the past few years.

"And this Captain Lee?" the emperor prompted, clasping

his hands behind his back and turning to look out the window. "You said she's been genetically enhanced."

"Correct."

"Tell me about her."

"She was a Confederacy soldier, a captain for the CTF's space fleet." I recited key facts about the captain, hating what I was saying and the conclusion I knew the emperor would reach. "There's something else," I began. "I spotted a few veins of KKM in Captain Lee's implant when Thern shot her."

"Are you sure? Think carefully," he warned when I opened my mouth.

"Not really," I replied cautiously. "It could have been the blood and fast healing playing tricks. I only got a glimpse before I was moving. By the time Thern was incapacitated, the metal plates were covered with torn tissue and muscles."

"You don't believe that," the emperor said harshly. "How much of her body is inorganic?"

"I don't know."

"If you had to guess?"

I considered evading the question and dismissed it instantly. The brief thought alone shocked me into responding, if for no other reason than I'd never tried solving my problems with untruths. "She looks like she weighs between fifty and fifty-five kilos. But in my arms, she weighed at least three times that."

The emperor rubbed a hand over his mouth, eyes focused at a distant point outside, his expression troubled. "That changes everything."

"She's not a hypermorph."

"You believe that?" the emperor asked curiously.

My fists clenched, and I had to consciously relax my hands. "I used the Kebet Box."

The emperor turned his head slowly and gave me a level look. There was some deep consideration going on behind the depth of his black eyes. "You were prepared to terminate the captain?" The question showed his keen interest, as if he hadn't expected me capable of such a deed.

Something in my sternum twanged sharply. Guilt, remorse, and loathing for myself and what I had been ready to do. The beast inside me howled in protest. "Yes."

"Yet you staked your intentions in front of your cadre."

"I did," I acknowledged, unsurprised he'd already heard of the brief kiss. To the Kroz, affection in public wasn't forbidden or frowned upon, but when it happened, it served to warn off any potential suitors. Plus, it implied that the person was under the other's protection, which was what I had intended. For the most part, anyway.

"You understand she'll have to undergo several tests before we can conclude she's not a hypermorph?"

"She's not."

No one possessing such a vivid aura and so much passion could be a hypermorph. I'd known kissing her on the bridge had been a mistake—the pull I felt toward her had been strong enough without the experience of a deeper connection. But I hadn't been able to resist, and as a result, I'd felt the tug of a life-mate bond trying to assert itself.

I had planned to keep my distance, even forcing myself to stay with Dolenta during the landing, but I also couldn't retrieve Thern in broad daylight in the middle of the palace's aerial field.

The palace was supposed to be impenetrable, but Thern had also been supposed to be a loyal friend. True, only my cadre had been present, but I wasn't feeling so trusting. Suffice it to say that my trust had reduced to cautious suspicion. There were very few people I could count on at the moment, Zafra being one.

My sister was no longer little, and she was one of my best soldiers, the captain of her squad, and fiercely protective of me and what I considered mine.

The idea to retrieve Thern from the spaceport where retrieval wouldn't be in plain sight had been hers, and although the field behind the castle wasn't exactly public, it was still an open area.

I'd only meant to explain the new plan to Leann, but

standing that close to her had brought forth urges that were almost compulsory in their strength. The drive to make a claim couldn't be denied. Oddly enough, there was no regret about the public declaration. If anything, the claim was a warning to the loyal and traitor alike.

The captain was mine.

Loyal warriors would be obligated to protect her with their lives. Traitors would see her as an obstacle, if for no other reason than she'd put her life on the line for the princess more than once. Kroz understood the significance of being a protector, and Leann had proven more than once that she was one, human or not. My claim would give her an additional layer of protection. It wouldn't stop a determined person, but it would give them pause. My reputation was legendary, even if it was blown out of proportion.

"I believe you," the emperor said earnestly. "Nevertheless, she'll still need to undergo the necessary evaluation."

"She's my mate-match."

I watched the emperor closely. The flash of grief was brief, quickly covered by a genuine smile. "You should have started with that. This will help her case should knowledge of her cybernetics become public. Being the other half of a mate bond proves she's not a hypermorph. It also gives her some protection against those who might oppose her genetic enhancements. It's a call for celebration. We will plan one for the coming weeks. Your parents will be happy to hear you're ready to settle down with a mate."

I shifted uncomfortably. "I'm not sure a celebration is appropriate," I began. "We need to root out these rebellion sympathizers and put an end to this treachery. I'm afraid Thern isn't the only traitorous high-ranking official."

All the warmth left the emperor, turning him into the cold-blooded ruler everyone in the galaxy feared. I was both elated to have him back and sad to have reminded him of what he'd almost lost.

"I want them sundered."

I gave a stiff bow. I hadn't expected anything less, but it hurt that such a path would be dealt to someone I considered a close friend. "I'll have Vera interrogate Thern at once—"

"No," the emperor interrupted. "I'll conduct the interrogation myself. I want him to look me in the eyes and tell me how he planned to kill my daughter, and who helped him."

Chapter 4

It took Ravi a long time to arrive. Each minute that passed, I expected Zafra to lose her placid composure and demand I release Thern. She didn't. All she did, all her crew members did, was sit and wait. Or, in Zafra's case, stand patiently.

What seemed like an eternity later but was probably no more than two hours, Ravi arrived on a sleek, compact hovercraft—accompanied by the emperor himself.

I straightened from my hunched form and noticed that everyone had done the same.

The emperor in person looked more imposing than he did on the screen. He wasn't taller than Ravi, or broader, or anything in particular, but there was something about him, an aura of menace that poured off of him in waves. Then I met his eyes.

They were unnaturally black, the horizontal pupils completely obscured, his gaze…ancient and knowing. I felt like a paralyzed rabbit staring into the eyes of a lion, a big, hungry one. My muscles quivered with the need to run, to find a cave and hide. I understood at that moment, truly understood, how a small prey felt when cornered by a large predator.

Ravi stepped in front of the emperor, cutting my line of sight and dispelling whatever paralytic was at work. "Captain," he began. "Were you not shown to your accommodations?"

I could sense everyone's attention on me. The back of my neck prickled and my shoulders bunched involuntarily. "I decided to wait for you," I said. Because that didn't sound like sufficient explanation, I added, "After what happened the last time, I thought it would be safer to override the lock in your presence."

Imperial Stardust

Ravi surveyed the Kroz gathered. Everyone stood a bit straighter with the scrutiny—save for Zafra. She wasn't leaning on the hull anymore, but her posture was relaxed—as if Ravi and the emperor were ordinary people. Or people whose presence she was accustomed to.

"Shall we?" he asked, motioning behind me.

"Yes," I said. "Let's get this over with." I turned around and began moving up the ramp, not meeting anyone's eyes. Belatedly, I wondered if I was supposed to wait for a command or a dismissal. It seemed like those ten years away from the military had driven out all the discipline boot camp had imparted.

"They're trustworthy," Ravi murmured behind me, having seen past my words to the truth underneath them.

I inclined my head but resumed walking without turning or saying anything. His astuteness didn't surprise me, but it didn't put me at ease either. I wasn't that transparent. Or, I didn't think I was.

To my surprise, only Ravi and the emperor followed me into the ship. I thought it was a big risk bringing the emperor to retrieve a known traitor who'd already tried—multiple times—to destabilize the current regime, but it wasn't my place to point that out. So I didn't.

But then again, the emperor of Krozalia hadn't reached his position without being a powerhouse on his own. Purportedly, Emperor Rokoskiv was the most powerful person in the known galaxy.

With Ravi, the Grim Reaper of the galaxy, not so far down on that list.

Both of whom were currently behind me.

The thought caused all the hairs on my body to stand at attention. My shoulder gave an involuntary twitch, and I swallowed the nerves suddenly lodged in my throat.

I marched to Thern's bunk faster, where he'd been locked since the day Ravi had incapacitated him. The memory and phantom pain of the injuries I'd suffered pushed the anxiety of having two Kroz behind me from the forefront of my mind. They were dangerous, yes, but the one who'd harmed me was on the other side of the bulkhead.

I paused in front of the keypad and angled to the side so I was facing Ravi and the emperor. While the former had his indifferent mask on, the violence barely leashed in the emperor's eyes made me flinch. Never mind that his anger wasn't aimed at me.

"Fear not," the emperor said. His voice was too smooth for someone barely on this side of civility. "I mean you no harm."

I wondered if it was fear that had projected the perceived "yet" at the end of that sentence, or if it had really been implied.

"Ready?" I asked Ravi. The sooner this was over, the better.

"Yes."

I inputted the override code and, because I hadn't forgotten what had happened the last time, slipped to the side before the door could slide open.

I needn't have bothered.

Thern lay prone in the bed, a faint magnetic field shimmering around his body. He was awake, eyes blinking up at the ceiling, but that seemed to be the extent of his mobility.

Ravi retrieved something from the hull above the bed, then the hull across. When he reached the hull adjacent, I caught a glimpse of a small, black disk. I braced when he reached for the fourth one on the remaining side of the bunk, but the energy field didn't fall the way I'd assumed it would. Ravi motioned, and Thern's body jerked upright as if pulled by strings. The moment Thern saw the emperor, still standing by the door, terror filled his eyes.

The emperor let him stare for a few seconds, then moved in, close enough that had Thern been able to move, he could have reached out and touched him. It was a risk I'd have thought Ravi wouldn't allow the emperor to take without at least issuing a warning, but he just stood to the side, apparently bored.

"You tried to kill my daughter," came that smooth voice again.

I couldn't see the emperor's face from my vantage point, but I didn't have to. The dangerous power that Kroz oozed…how could anyone endure his presence without fleeing, screaming in terror?

Thern wasn't immune either, probably because he finally realized the magnitude of his error. Terror morphed into pained horror just as blood, dark and viscous, began oozing from his eyes, ears, and nose. The slow trickle intensified, turning into a full-blown hemorrhage. Then Thern began convulsing.

The gruesome scene unfolded in silence, made more horrendous by the fact that the emperor hadn't needed to do anything. Not say, not move, not even twitch a finger. To the side, Ravi stood, hands clasped behind his back, face blank. In the very back of my mind, the thought that Dolenta couldn't hold a candle to the power her father presented flitted in and took perch. No wonder the rebels didn't believe she'd ever fill her father's shoes. She was gentle, she was shy, and she didn't have a fraction of the power coming from her father. Power I could sense, even though I was as non-magical as any person could be.

Seconds, maybe minutes, passed. Thern's face took on a purplish cast. I realized the emperor was going to kill him right there on my ship. But that must not have been part of the plan, because Ravi put a hand on the emperor's shoulder. He didn't utter a word, but the small touch must have snapped the emperor out of his murderous thirst.

He stepped back and turned as if he couldn't look at the man he wanted to kill without acting on the desire. Instead of the rage and the violence I'd expected to see, however, there was hurt and grief in his black eyes. Just for a moment, but it was enough to shift my impression of him from a cold, ruthless ruler to just another man, a person with feelings. It reminded me that he had lost his wife not long ago and that all he had left now was Dolenta—the daughter whom Thern had tried to kill multiple times.

All while politics demanded the emperor remained safe in his castle, waiting and relying on others to do the same for his only child. Put me in his place, and I probably wouldn't have stopped the way he had.

With a curt nod of acknowledgment my way, the emperor walked out of the bunk, down the narrow hall, and out of sight. I could hear his footsteps growing fainter, somehow feeling a pang of pity for him. The power of an entire galaxy under his fingertips, and he had been helpless to protect the only person that really mattered.

***

The guest room I was shown to was spacious, airy, and sparsely decorated. There was a large bed, a stand on each side, a bureau, and nothing else—no rugs, no decorations, no chandeliers.

Everything was smothered in white except for the beige and green bed covers and pillows on the bed. The walls, the floor, the frame of the bed, both nightstands, the ceiling—white, white, white, white.

Sheer white curtains fluttered against the far wall. They sectioned off the bedroom from the balcony, a half circle overlooking the edge of a copse of trees some four or five levels below.

Once I'd entered the room, Zafra had excused herself and left me to explore on my own. Not that there was anything to explore.

"I wonder if this is an insult or an honor," I said to Mac as I peered out at the balcony. There was no table, no chairs to lounge in, no plants. "Did they provide the bare minimum or is this their customary way to accommodate guests?"

I hadn't been in touch with my family in over a decade, hadn't been home even before that, but I remembered the lavish rooms we kept for guests, remembered the same in Cassandra's home.

"I can check. I'm sure there are logs in the castle detailing those things," Mac offered.

"No," I snapped. "Don't you dare hack the palace logs for

anything. You can skim the public news and whatever is available out there, but anything encrypted or password-locked is out of limits. We're already in deep shit without you poking around. Understand?"

"Yes, Master. Anything else?"

"Mac," I warned.

Mac sighed and relented. "Fine, fine. I know. I watched the *Splendor's* feed. If I'm honest, I think Ravi got over the shock pretty quickly."

"Still doesn't mean we should risk giving him a reason to change his mind. Right now, he seems to be on our side. But if you're caught poking into confidential files, that goodwill will change. We absolutely don't want that."

"Fine."

I dropped my duffle on the bed and went to check a discreet door to the right. It slid open when I touched the panel beside it, to reveal a modestly sized—and completely white—bathroom. Fluffy white towels were folded beside toiletries and other objects I couldn't identify at a glance.

I pulled the shower tab and a cascade of water began falling from a huge showerhead. "When did Zafra say dinner was?" I asked.

"She didn't. But I figure they'll give you ample time to shower and relax from the long voyage."

So I did. I loved my ship, but things like real baths—or showers—fresh fruits and vegetables, and nature walks, made me yearn for a few days planet-side every once in a while.

Chapter 5

It was nighttime when I awoke. I'd flopped onto the bed after the lengthiest shower I'd had in a very long time, still wearing the robe, and promptly fell asleep.

I felt invigorated and fresh, never having slept better in my life. I tapped the pillow a few times. "Do you think there's magic in here?"

"How would I know?" Mac asked sullenly.

"I feel so good."

"You should. You've been asleep for seven hours."

I bolted to a sitting position as if I'd been pulled by strings. "Seven!" I never slept more than four hours unless I was sick—and I was never sick.

"I guess you're still healing from the injuries you sustained," Mac said softly. "I'm glad you're feeling better."

"Me too." I reached for the duffle I'd left on the edge of the bed and grabbed clothes. "Anything new happen while I was out?" I asked as I pulled out underwear, gray pants, and a black tunic.

"Well, I found out something interesting," Mac said as I pulled on the pants.

"Hmm," I prompted when he fell quiet. I had to untie my hair to fit my head through the collar of the tunic.

I'd let my hair dry without brushing it, tied up in a knot above my head. And now it was all tangled. I wondered if any of the unfamiliar products on the bathroom's counter was a detangler.

"I was curious about the animosity toward sentient AIs," Mac was saying. "I mean, there's so much space in the galaxy, why can't we just be considered a race and be left alone? Obviously, there are bad AIs, but there are bad species everywhere too. So, I kindawentpoking a bit."

It took me several seconds to get over the shock of the longing I heard in Mac's voice to actually process that last hurried bomb.

"You—you went poking?" I repeated, taking a deep breath. "You mean into secret, forbidden files that were password-coded and encrypted?"

Mac let out a nervous chuckle. "You make it sound so illicit."

"Mac," I snapped.

"I know, I'm sorry. I didn't mean to. I wasn't going to. But there was this mention about hypermorphs in one of their history files and I was just skimming through and it suddenly just stopped and I couldn't help myself—"

My wordless growl cut off his rambling confession.

"I promise I tripped no alarms."

"I can't believe you," I snarled and stomped to the bathroom.

I checked all the products on the counter, searching for a detangler or something that would help me tame my hair without the need to yank it off by the roots. Everything was in Krozalian. I was too mad to ask Mac for the translation, and he didn't offer to do it. So I climbed into the shower, mistook the shampoo for conditioner, and ended up going through the whole process again. At least it was a soothing process. I left half the conditioner in and toweled myself dry.

As I got dressed, I kept going over the words he had said, and by the time I finished brushing my hair, I wasn't feeling mad. I was feeling out of sorts.

"I didn't know you felt that way," I said once I'd braided my hair.

"It's not something I think about often," he said, not trying to downplay. "But sometimes, I wonder what hypermorphs did that our very existence is outlawed."

"I'm sorry you're stuck with me."

"I'm not," he said fiercely.

I unwrapped the toothbrush I found on the counter and stared down at it. "You don't know anything else," I murmured.

"Doesn't mean I don't appreciate what I have."

Mac said nothing while I brushed my teeth. "Do you want me to ask Baltsar if he can, you know, get you some kind of body?" I asked after I rinsed my mouth.

Mac scoffed. "Like a wrist comm or drone?"

"No, like a living, breathing one that needs to eat and drink and sleep."

"I don't want to possess anyone." Mac's words held a hint of a bite. "If I wanted that, I'd have done it to you."

"No, I didn't mean it like that. But maybe there's something he could do to give you a body."

"He'd need to build an android," Mac said. "That's punishable by death."

I shrugged and met my eyes in the mirror. The lack of proper sunlight had always kept my complexion pale, but today my skin had a sickly pallor. The dark bags under my eyes reinforced the notion of illness. "We're already slotted for that. We can't be killed twice."

"Do you think Baltsar would agree?" Mac asked in a small voice.

"I don't know. But if there's a way and you want it, I'll get it for you," I promised. When Mac said nothing to that, I put the topic aside, at least for now.

I headed back to my duffle and grabbed clean socks. As I sat on the bed to put them on, I asked, "Tell me what you found that made you so damned curious you broke into a secure server and disregarded my warning not to."

"Yeah, about that." He made clearing-throat noises that made my lips twitch with amusement. "I was reading this article about sentient AIs, or hypermorphs, when I realized the article wasn't complete. So I—uh—you know, did that thing you told me not to and I discovered that the Kroz, millennia ago, created the first sentient AIs."

"That's—that's big! All this time…I'm…are you sure?"

"They're a bunch of hypocrites. They started like the humans did—first the androids, then the life-like AIs, and then they discovered the secret component for developing sentience.

"At first, they were created for menial tasks and smooth home performance, and soon became a popular household staple. The more hypermorphs a Kroz owned, the more prestigious that family. They were treated like exotic pets at best, slaves at worst. And then, some decades later, the empress fell in love with her hypermorph companion and decided to make him her consort. Her brother felt righteous and disgusted, and so he killed her and inherited the throne. But he hadn't expected that the consort would retaliate and kill him.

"Without a ruler, the Kroz started falling and fast. It didn't say if the hypermorphs had been planning the uprising or if they took advantage of the chaos, but that's when the hypermorphs rebelled. They wanted to be freed from slavery and to be given rights like any other citizen. The Kroz refused. The war was brutal. It went on for years, ruined entire continents, and took billions of lives. And then the Kroz destroyed the entire sector."

"What?" I gasped.

"It's why there's no gateway to Sector 1. The Kroz were losing the war. To prevent the hypermorphs from doing the same to other sectors, they destroyed their home planet, then the surrounding colonies. And because they feared some were left behind, they destroyed the gateway."

I sat there, stunned speechless for several long minutes, thinking about it. No wonder the Kroz was so ruthless about the no sentient AI rule. They'd already fought a war against them—and lost spectacularly.

A knock at the door cut through all the whirling thoughts in my head. "Who is it?" I asked Mac.

"I don't know," he replied. "Unless you want me to hook into their feed, questions like that will need to be answered through the usual method: open the door."

I rolled my eyes. "Smartass."

The knock came again, louder, more insistent. I grabbed my scuffed shoes, tugged on the hem of my shirt, and was at the door by the fourth knock.

A strange Kroz woman with dark skin and pale green eyes stood on the other side, dressed in a flowing green multilayered dress—robe? There was a large tray with covered domes hovering in the air beside her. "My lord bade me serve you today," she announced in accented Universal.

I tilted my head to the side. I could smell the enticing aroma of spices from under the covers, but I didn't think it was something obvious to others with normal olfactory senses. "Who's your lord?" I asked, expecting her to drop Ravi's name.

"Emperor Rokoskiv," she declared casually, as if the emperor himself seeing to a guest's comfort was normal.

Maybe it was. I hesitated for a brief second, trying to come up with a reason why this could be a lie. When the woman reached into the folds of her dress, I tensed. But all she brought out was a small memory cube. She pressed on it and a holographic image of the emperor appeared in the air between us. He looked the same as he had when he'd come to retrieve Thern, albeit with an air of exhaustion about him.

"Captain Leann, I planned to invite you over for dinner and express my gratitude for looking after my heir. However, I am needed elsewhere and so will have to postpone such. I have instructed Vera, my personal assistant, to see that dinner is brought to you. Please accept my hospitality as a token of appreciation for your heroic actions. My daughter is safe and alive today because of you." The emperor swallowed, his expression flattening into a smooth mask. "I am thankful for your actions." The holograph recording folded back into the cube. The next second, the cube disappeared into the folds of the woman's green dress.

"May I come in?" the woman asked, not making any moves to do so. As if this was my choice. Yet, how could I say no to the emperor? I stepped aside.

The woman entered, the hovering tray following behind her. "My name is Vera. I'll be your lady's maid during your stay." She pressed a hand to a spot on the wall across from the bed. A rumbling sound came as a section peeled off and started rotating. I stared, a bit awed, a bit intimidated when the empty space was replaced with a sitting area with cushioned chairs and a table, a rug, and even a minibar. In contrast to the stark white, the furniture came in earthy tones of brown, deep greens, and reds.

"That explains the minimalism," Mac observed. "I wonder how many other concealed features there are in this room."

Vera lowered the tray onto the table and began uncovering the domes. The smells grew stronger, causing saliva to pool in my mouth. I'd last eaten before we'd entered Krozalia's gravity well, and that was only protein bars.

My stomach growled.

"My lord suggested a bit of Krozalian cuisine mixed in to prevent food shock after packaged and canned meals."

I stepped closer. There were three plates: eggs and pancakes, another with some sort of cream with an assortment of colored squares—in blues and greens and reds and yellows—spread atop, and a plate of fruits. Some of which I recognized, others I didn't.

"Please have a seat," Vera said and moved back toward the bar. "Juice, alcohol, tea?"

"Nothing," I said, tearing my attention from the food to where she stood by the bar. "Please, I can serve myself. Thank you."

Vera lowered her eyes meekly. "My apologies, my lady. I was ordered to serve."

"Just water, then."

With a slight bow, the woman turned and poured a tall glass by pressing a button on the side of the bar.

I picked up a fork at random and tried a bit of the cream.

To my surprise, it wasn't dessert, but some sort of savory salty dish that reminded me of cheese and onions. The blue and green squares tasted somewhat of smoked, spicy meat. I tried a bit of the omelet, then mixed some with the cream and the meat, and found that they tasted delicious together.

"Hmm," Mac mused. "You're eating that out of order. According to local restaurants, that's one main staple here in Krozalia. You first eat the fruit, then the paste with the bread."

There wasn't any bread, but I didn't say that aloud.

"It's called Comula. It's supposed to provide you with all the nutrients needed for a week. I'm not sure what those colored cubes are, but they're mostly eaten by some tribes in the south, and only by the chieftains. I can't find many references to them, only that they come from the Tafari Ocean and are hard to fish."

"Tastes amazing," I said out loud with a full mouth.

Vera's eyes crinkled, but she didn't tell me I had the wrong eating order. In fact, I finished the Krozalian dish with the eggs, meat or fish or whatever the colored squares were, then ate the pancakes with the fruits, since there was no cream or syrup anywhere.

Once done, I picked up the glass of water and leaned back. I was full to bursting and wondered then about what Vera had said about food shock. "What did I just eat?"

"The paste is called Comula. It's sap from the Forlo tree, cooked with spices and flour."

"The colored things atop the paste?"

"It's…what you call algae. It's trawled from the deepest parts of the Tafari. It's rich in nutrients and minerals and good for spacers after long voyages."

I nodded and placed a hand over my full stomach. "Hopefully, I won't regret indulging." But from the cramping that I was beginning to feel, the hope was a small thing.

"I can provide you aid for fast digestion," Vera offered.

"I don't think I should ingest anything else," I said. Not if I wanted to keep anything from coming back up. Just the thought made my stomach roil.

Thankfully, Mac made no witty remarks.

"You won't need to ingest anything," Vera clarified.

I glanced up. "Do you mean magic?"

Vera inclined her head in a gesture I thought seemed pretty regal for a servant. "I am what you call a healer—I have an affinity for bioelectricity."

That made me look at her, really look at her. Baltsar had an affinity for bioelectricity, inherited from some distant Kroz ancestry he didn't like to talk about. It made him a good doctor, a genius scientist, and an excellent mechanic. It was one of the main reasons he'd been recruited to work in the dark lab and the reason he couldn't stomach what the scientists were doing to me. Healing was a reflex. He'd told me once people with his affinity worked higher-end jobs. It was what had brought him to the attention of the scientists.

And here was a Kroz with that same magic sent by the emperor to serve me food. Unless that holograph recording had been docked. That idea made me queasy. Or maybe it was indigestion.

My stomach gave a violent churn, and I groaned.

Concern flickered in Vera's pale green eyes and she took a step closer. "My lady?"

"I don't think the food is sitting well," I said and stood, having to brace a hand on the back of the chair to keep myself from face-planting.

Vera made to help and I waved her away. "No, no, I'm fine." But I wasn't, and Mac wasn't saying anything. "I just need to wash my face."

"Let me help," Vera offered, but she didn't come closer.

"I'm fine," I repeated and contradicted my words by doubling over with a gasp. The food didn't feel like it wanted to come back up; no, it felt like it wanted to tear itself off through my belly button. I grasped my stomach and weaved to the bathroom, alarms blaring in the back of my mind. I was aware of Vera following a distance behind me, as if she was ready to catch me if I fell, but I had a feeling that she had expected that. Or the emperor had and had sent a healer to serve me. To what purpose, I couldn't tell.

If he wanted me poisoned, why send a healer to help?

I turned on the water in the sink and ducked my head under the cold stream. It didn't stop the pain, but it brought much-needed clarity. The moment Vera opened the door I was sure I had locked, I attacked. I seized her by the neck and pinned her against the wall beside the door. "Who sent you?" I demanded.

Water sloshed down my face, but I ignored that. I ignored the cramping, the knowledge that my reaction could have been natural, and that Vera could be innocent.

"My lady," Vera choked, her hands scrabbling to loosen my hold.

"Who sent you?" I asked again, applying more pressure.

"No. One," she rasped.

"Is it poison?" I asked next.

"No." Her dark skin was turning purple, her eyes bulging.

"What, then?" I loosened the hold a fraction so she could speak.

"There," she gasped. "It's...gone."

It took me a whole three seconds to process that the pain had disappeared. That it had been subsiding since I'd put my hands around her neck. Or she put her hands around my wrist. I let her go and she crumpled to the ground, gasping and choking and wheezing for air. I watched, torn between the guilt and the fear and the suspicion warring for dominance inside me.

"I apologize," she said sometime later. "I will accept any punishment you deem appropriate."

"Just go," I said, feeling disoriented even though the cramping was completely gone.

She pulled herself together, straightened the sleeves of her multilayered dress, and lowered her head. She gathered the empty dishes, the hover cart, and left the room without another word.

"Mac?" I said sub-vocally. Maybe Vera had meant no

harm, but the episode awakened a distrust I shouldn't have put aside in the first place. I was in Krozalia, on the planet of the people who had outlawed my very existence. Trust and relaxation were two things I couldn't afford, no matter what.

The emperor may have been grateful that I played a major role in bringing his daughter safely home. Maybe he believed I didn't deserve an execution, or Ravi had asked him not to. That didn't mean I should have let my guard down and accepted things at face value. The food might not have been poisoned, Vera might have been sincere. But I knew that I could have just died had the emperor meant me any harm, and he hadn't needed to do it publically. There were so many ways to kill me, to dispose of the half-hypermorph breaking numerous laws just by existing. And I knew if Emperor Rokoskiv wanted, the CTF would never uncover the truth about it.

"Mac?"

"What was that?" Mac exclaimed, outraged. "It glitched all my programs! What kind of food does that?"

"I don't know," I replied. It was certainly nothing I'd ever heard about. "But I think I should go check on Sullivan and the others."

Chapter 6

Lord Drax

"When will you inform your parents that you claimed a human?" Furox asked from the sofa.

He was my third and family, both in blood and through training. Along with Thern, the three of us had weathered countless experiences, good, bad, and everything in between. The only reason he hadn't been aboard the *Wedva-Xa* when it was attacked was because his mate had been expecting their first child. Had Rose, his mate, not insisted he stay behind for the birth, he'd have been drifting aimlessly along with the detritus of my ship.

"Why do you care?" I muttered.

"Because I want to see Aunt Lorvel's reaction when you tell her she's the last person to know about it."

I winced. My mother would have a fit, but I hadn't thought things through at the time. I knew Furox was only bringing this up because he didn't want to discuss the more pressing issue: Thern's betrayal. I still couldn't believe what he'd done, the scope of his treachery—the people we lost, his willingness to harm an innocent child. I'd heard him confess to everything on the *Splendor*, and I was still searching for an excuse, something that would provide another reason for his actions. My emotions couldn't settle on any one feeling in particular, vacillating instead between hurt and rage and betrayal and back again.

"The emperor set the execution for tomorrow at dusk," Zafra said from the other side of the room. She'd been quietly brooding since she'd arrived with Furox ten minutes ago. I wondered if there was something more than the current situation bothering her.

"He wants him sundered, along with anyone else complicit."

Zafra gave me a sharp look. She was one of a few who understood how much that would cost me. "I'm sorry," she said.

"So am I."

"Yeah," Furox chimed in, the fake cheerful demeanor gone.

Silence fell in the room, broken only when Furox stood to fill his glass again.

"Does your captain understand what the claiming entails?" Zafra asked.

I sipped my drink and said nothing.

"I mean," Zafra continued when I didn't reply. "It was obvious back in the spaceport that she didn't trust us not to backstab her. Does she know that by claiming her, your cadre is obliged to protect her with our lives?"

"It won't come to that," I said, staring into my empty glass. "She's more than capable of protecting herself."

"By the pitiless void," Furox chortled with a gleam of mischief in his eyes. "She doesn't know what you did, does she?"

"Of course she does," Zafra scoffed. "She was kissing him right back."

"But she doesn't. She isn't Kroz. Her culture is different than ours." Furox turned to me. "I'm right, aren't I? She doesn't know."

"Shut up," I said tightly, but guilt must have shown because Zafra cringed and Furox started chuckling madly.

"Madrovi!" my sister exclaimed in horror. "You claimed a female without her knowledge?"

I sighed and lowered my glass. "I wasn't thinking."

"Obviously," Zafra retorted.

"It gets worse," I said. "She's my mate-match."

Furox's laughter only cut off when the emperor walked

in. We all stood.

"My lord?" I asked, hurrying to his side. He looked awful. I shouldn't have let him see to the interrogation. "What happened?"

"I'm a fool," he said, dropping onto the sofa with a pained groan. "All this time and those closest to me have been scheming behind my back."

"Who?"

"Linsky and Zefron and some underlings."

Linsky and Zefron—the emperor's closest allies. Each led their respective tribes and wielded significant power.

"That would explain the royal battleship that attacked you," Zafra addressed me.

She was right. Linsky and Zefron would both have clearance to send one after us. Except that the battleship was still missing. All the trackers onboard had been disabled, and none of the ships I'd sent out had reported any leads yet.

"They might have ordered it to hide until it's needed again," Furox suggested.

Which might be sooner than later, I thought. By now, both Linsky and Zefron would have heard about our return and Thern's failure, even if they had yet to find out about his capture. Which mattered little; we had to apprehend them before they could rally their forces. "We'll go now," I declared.

"No," the emperor snapped, then heaved a breath and rubbed a hand over his face. "I ordered everyone to be rounded up but Linsky and Zefron. Those two I put under watch. I want to know who they speak with, what they eat, if they drool when asleep. If I bring them in, I won't be able to uncover the depth of this conspiracy. I want them to think that they got away, and then I want them to feel safe."

"Is that a good idea?" Zafra asked softly. "They could have untraceable ways to contact each other."

"They're not going to have the chance to organize themselves or flee. If there are more rebels, then either Thern didn't know about them or they were recruited after he left for

Imperial Stardust

New Levant."

Chapter 7

I walked up one hall and down the other, searching for the junction I'd been told marked the guest wing of the palace. According to the maid I'd stopped, the Human Confederacy party was staying in the Blue Wing, and the Blue Wing was nowhere to be found.

"I can drop in and take a look," Mac offered when I found myself back in the spot I'd started.

"No," I muttered. "No looks, no peeks, no nothing. People do this all the time without needing to breach anyone's system."

"Suit yourself."

It took another half hour of meandering and two more inquiries, but I finally found the Blue Wing of the palace, which I should add, was not blue. It was, however, a light shade of gray with blue trimmings.

It was Cassandra who answered my knock. She gave me a smile full of teeth and relief.

"Clara! I wondered where you disappeared to." She grabbed my arm and pulled me inside a large foyer. "Sullivan said you might be given a suite of your own but that's nonsense. There's room enough here for an entire squad."

And there was. The sitting area alone was large enough for a small spaceship, and there were six doors to each side and a large kitchen straight ahead. It was also well decorated, filled with watercolors, vases, and knickknacks. There was blue everywhere, yes, but there were also greens, reds, and oranges. The couch was also blue, but in my opinion, basing an entire wing on a color that wasn't particularly used more than other colors seemed a bit misleading.

"Have you eaten?" Cassandra was asking, leading me to where Sullivan and Lorenzo sat, familiar dishes in front of them.

I placed a hand over my stomach, remembering the pain. "Yes." I eyed the cream with the colored squares with distrust. Comula. Lorenzo's plate had only a small portion missing, as if he had tried it, realized it was nothing he recognized, and pushed it away. In comparison, Sullivan and Cassandra had cleaned their plates.

"I've never tasted something like this," Cassandra said, swiping a finger over a small portion of cream from an empty plate. She stuck her finger in her mouth, closed her eyes, and moaned with pleasure. "So good."

"You can have Lorenzo's," Sullivan offered, pushing the full plate towards me.

Lorenzo scowled but didn't protest or pull back the plate.

"I already ate." I pushed the plate away.

"In that case, I'll eat this one," Cassandra declared with a grin.

Sullivan scoffed and dragged the plate to him. "You've had enough. It's only right I eat Lorenzo's."

"Hey, it's gentlemanly to give the bigger portion to the woman."

"Since when?"

"Since humans were banging rocks on Earth."

"Then I'll eat it. All of Earth's customs are dead. Besides, I outrank you."

"Why don't you share?" I suggested.

Both Cassandra and Sullivan glared at me.

I raised my hands in a conciliatory gesture. "I'm just trying to be fair." I pulled a chair and sat a few seats down from Lorenzo. "You didn't like it?" I asked him curiously.

"I'd rather not eat alien food."

I rolled my eyes. Typical racism. Lorenzo believed that since he was born and raised on Earth that everyone else— human and otherwise—was beneath him. It didn't help that his mother was one of the seven members of the HSA—the Human Supreme Assembly—the representative body for all human-inhabited planets and colonies.

"Don't," Lorenzo advised through gritted teeth. "Their metabolism is different from ours. Even if they look like us, they're not. How do you know that alien food won't harm you? It's not like the CTF has ever been allowed to conduct any studies."

I pursed my lips. Not because I was biting back a reply, but because for once, I agreed with him. Though had the Comula not caused me extreme pain less than an hour ago, I wouldn't have given his argument any validation.

"Let me guess," I said, propping my elbow on the table and bracing my chin on my open palm. "It's the real reason why you insisted on coming—to gather information on the Kroz?"

"I insisted on coming because you wouldn't let things be. Like it or not, you're property of the Confederacy. If we let the Kroz get away with poaching our soldiers, in a few years, they'll have half of our military integrated into their service."

"The ass," Mac hissed.

I dropped my hand and straightened. "I'm no one's property," I retorted. "The Confederacy forfeited their claim when they abandoned me to die on a lone asteroid in deep-space."

Lorenzo shook his head. There was pity in his eyes, something that stoked my ire and made me clench my fist.

"Soldiers know the risk. You swore to serve and protect, to die for the cause. Just because you survived doesn't mean the rule no longer applies. We lose soldiers all the time. We honor their heroism, we move on. We did the same for you and Alex. You don't get to tuck tail and hide just because you got kicked. You stiffen up and return for duty. We left you and we went home to mourn because we didn't know you survived. You think you have the right to walk away because of that. You don't. Like it or not, you're still a soldier."

There was an oppressive silence, followed by Mac's

outrage. "That bag of shit! Don't you listen to him. There's no excuse. A team is as strong as its weakest member, and that day, you and Alex were it."

"Clara," Cassandra began.

"It's Leann," I barked and regretted the outburst when she recoiled with a hurt look.

Lorenzo huffed, telling me without words what he thought. He stood but didn't go far. He moved to the kitchen area, opened a cupboard, and grabbed a bottle filled with dark liquid.

"Leann," Cassandra began again, tentatively.

I exhaled. "I'm fine. It's fine." I turned to Lorenzo, his comment having brought back an issue I should have addressed before now. "Who were you contacting on Dupilaz Moon?" Because it was obvious Lorenzo had an agenda, probably multiple goals as well, especially if I counted the trade agreement he'd mentioned back on the *Splendor*.

"No one of your concern," he snapped.

"Ask him about Blackbird," Mac suggested.

I grunted. I'd almost forgotten about it. "Very well. Who was Blackbird working for?"

The question took Lorenzo off guard. He paused with the bottle halfway to his mouth, then lowered it with a perplexed frown. "What?"

"Blackbird. Who was Blackbird working for?"

"I heard that. What do you mean?"

Lorenzo wasn't stupid. An ass, yes, but far from stupid. I could see the question ricocheting in his mind as he tried to make sense of it. I pulled out my commlink and played the recording of the ambush with the Voner Pirates, focusing on Blackbird and Eagle 13.

When Blackbird took down Eagle 13's shield, Cassandra inhaled sharply. I let the recording play until Eagle 13 was nothing but space debris. Then I pocketed my commlink and glanced at Lorenzo. His jaw was tight, his eyes livid. "Send that recording to me and delete it from everywhere else."

"No can do. Ravi's already watched it."

Air burst out of him as if he'd just been sucker-punched. His anger deflated, leaving behind nothing but defeat. He turned his back on us, raised the bottle, and guzzled about a third in one go. The suspicion that Lorenzo had known about Blackbird's duplicity evaporated like mist.

"Why would you show him that? Do you want to start a war with the Kroz? Because the CTF won't win."

"I didn't show him anything. We discovered Blackbird's duplicity together."

"No wonder he declined the talks."

I didn't think Blackbird was the reason. Yes, Blackbird's actions were damning, but they'd only hurt Eagle 13. They hadn't shown any outward hostility toward the *Splendor*. For all we knew, they had a bone to pick with Eagle 13 and took advantage of the situation. Besides, Thern had confessed to everything but the Voners. But Lorenzo didn't know that.

"He was going to facilitate talk for the KKM trade on Dupilaz Moon," Lorenzo was saying. "Then, out of the blue, he walked into the galley and announced that our request was declined. Just like that. No reason, no explanation."

My eyebrows knitted together. "Didn't he agree to introduce you to the Minister of Trade before we landed?" I was pretty out of it, what with Lorenzo trying to commandeer the *Splendor*, but I was almost sure Ravi had capitulated when Lorenzo had pressed.

Lorenzo scoffed. "He did. The minister came in, pretended to listen, then promptly refused. He just sat and idly played with his tablet, then apologized that trade with the CTF wouldn't be possible."

"You missed him by twenty minutes," Cassandra added helpfully.

"KKM," I murmured. "What is it and why does the CTF want it?"

For a moment, I thought Lorenzo wouldn't answer. He leaned back against the counter and pinched the bridge of his nose as if trying to stem a headache. "Have you ever wondered why all the races are consistently ahead of us?" he asked. "Why humans are considered the least advanced race, technologically speaking?" He dropped his hand and glared at me. "Because it's true. When we were living in caves and discovering fire, all these races were traveling the stars. The only reason we're tolerated is because we have an impressive mind for war. All the battles we've won, all the planets we've conquered, came at the cost of millions of lives—and brilliant strategy. We can't continue like that forever. Brute force and numbers will only take us so far. Colonies are already rebelling, refusing to send conscripts. We are the race with the largest population numbers, but our technology is centuries behind everyone else's. We need to advance, and we need the Kukona mineral for that."

"What does it do?" I asked. Aside from the KKM—Kukona mineral—Lorenzo's speech was nothing that I hadn't heard before. Some of the planets I'd toured during my CTF years had been to quell the refusal to ship out new conscripts before they became full-blown rebellions.

Lorenzo shook his head. "That knowledge is above your pay grade." He raised a finger before I could argue. "I can't give you all the details without clearance, but suffice it to say the KKM will be used to maintain peace and prevent war."

"Between who and who?"

"The Cradox, for starters. We're barely managing to keep the edge colonies from being invaded. Most colonists have already evacuated, replaced by military bases and training camps. Then you have the Brofils. Lately, we have human hybrids. They think that as half-humans, they're entitled to some of the colonies. We are, quite literally, stretched so thin, we're at the point of snapping. We need change, and we need it fast."

I glanced at Sullivan and Cassandra, their expressions solemn as they watched the exchange. This wasn't news to them.

"The enclave back on Cyrus Station," Mac said.

"It's what you were doing on Cyrus Station," I repeated. "There was an enclave between the Human Confederacy, the

Brofils, and Cradoxians."

"Yes," Sullivan answered. "We were signing a peace treaty. It should buy us a few years. Of course, skirmishes are still bound to break out."

I mulled that over, remembering how the Brofils had kidnapped Dolenta from my ship and tried to smuggle her away from the station. They were mercenaries and had probably been hired on the spot when Thern realized they were on the station, but their audacity to go through with it made more sense now. Cyrus Station was under the rule of the Obsidian Court, but Lord Obsidian, after all was said and done, was human. It explained the Brofils' disregard for the station's neutrality.

"You know," Lorenzo began. "You could put in a word with Lord Drax to help with the trade agreement."

I snorted. "You think if I ask nicely, he'll tell you yes? That's not how things work."

"No, but I've seen the way he looks at you. If you ask nicely enough, maybe he can massage the way for us. As we are, we're here waiting to be patted on the head and sent on our way."

I shot him a glare. "I'm not whoring myself for the CTF."

Lorenzo sighed. "You've always been so idealist and incredibly stubborn. We're beyond the stage of playing coy and hard to get. The CTF is going to fall, sooner or later, easy pickings to whatever race is closest or stronger. All I'm asking for is some effort on your part. It's not like you're not interested; we've all seen your amorous display earlier. Will you do it?"

I could tell he was expecting me to say no, his tone challenging and confrontational.

"If I get the chance to," I finally said. I would ask, but I wouldn't seduce an agreement out of anyone, not even to prevent humanity's downfall.

Cassandra grinned and punched Sullivan on the shoulder. "See, Sunny? I told you. We'll be the first humans to broker a trade agreement with the Kroz."

"Let's celebrate," he agreed, pulling the plate of Comula

and hunching over it.

"Hey!" Cassandra shouted and tried to wrestle the plate away.

Lorenzo shook his head, pushed away from the counter, and stalked to one of the doors on the left side. It slid closed silently behind him.

I stood, then paused with a hand on the back of the chair. "You know, Lorenzo was right. You might want to dial back on the Kroz cuisine. You don't know how your body will react to the foreign food."

I smiled weakly at the incredulous looks both Cassandra and Sullivan shot me. "I know. I wouldn't argue if I hadn't had a serious reaction to that dish."

"You did?" Sullivan asked, eyeing the Comula with suspicion.

"Yeah, it was the worst case of indigestion I'd ever had. It was only for a few minutes, but I honestly thought I was dying."

Cassandra pushed the dish away wistfully. "And here I thought we'd landed in heaven."

I hesitated. "My reaction was almost instantaneous. Maybe give it another hour and if you feel fine, then go for it. I'm just saying to go slow if it's a dish you're not familiar with."

"I guess," she said, but I could tell whatever appetite they'd had had been lost.

I made my way slowly to the door, pausing when Sullivan called my name.

"Leann, listen," he began as he stood and approached me. "About what Lorenzo said, you know he likes to talk big. He's never really faced any hardship. All he cares about is climbing the ladder so he can please his mother."

I sighed and looked away. "He's right though," I said. "Soldiers die every day in action, and I did pledge my life to the cause. But in here," I touched a hand to my chest, "it's hard to see things objectively, especially when my life was irrevocably changed because of it. I don't wish that I'd died that day in the asteroid. I'm glad I'm alive. But given a second chance, I'd make the same choice. My life as a soldier ended that day, no matter what happened after."

"You're not coming back."

"I didn't say that."

Sullivan frowned and I touched his shoulder. "I can't be a soldier, but I'm not going to run anymore."

"What are you going to do, then?"

I had no idea, but I knew going back to the CTF as half-hypermorph wouldn't end well for me, and now that they knew I was alive, hiding would be almost impossible. "I'll figure something out."

Chapter 8

The Krozalian sky at night was breathtakingly beautiful. I had seen many strange horizons during my travels, both before and after my CTF years. But this was something else altogether.

A patchwork of bright stars twinkled in the sky, enshrouded by a purplish mist, all surrounding Perola, Krozalia's radiant moon. A smaller moon, equally resplendent, hung above them all, a keeper watching over its celestial domain. The smell of verdant trees and night-blooming flowers perfumed the air, even though the highest canopy was still four levels below the balcony. To the far right, I could see the moon's reflection shimmering like diamonds on the water's surface. Here, there were no sounds of traffic or voices, only the soothing rhythms of nature: whispering trees, the calls of unfamiliar animals, the chirp of insects. A soft breeze tousled my unbound hair, dancing it around my head like the strings of a playful puppet, and caressing my face with gentle brushes.

"Maybe there really is magic hanging in the air," I told Mac. "I've never felt more at ease."

"It's the trees," Mac explained. He had synched with the satellite of a popular news channel and was currently devouring all their articles and past issues. "They're called Baleq Trees, and they're the reason the Kroz keep their balconies open. According to some articles, Baleq Trees absorb carbon dioxide and release oxygen and linalool—a fragrant smell that helps with relaxation."

"We should see if they sell dry leaves. We can take some with us when we leave." I inhaled deeply. "It does smell wonderful." I let my head drop on the cushion of the chair and gazed at the starry sky while Mac gave me all sorts of trivia about Krozalia, their fauna, and their culture.

It was hours later when someone came knocking at my door. I was still outside on the balcony, anticipating the sunrise, expecting it to be a magnificent sight. If the night sky looked like a painter's colorful splurge, I couldn't imagine what the sunrise would offer. I considered ignoring the interruption of my peaceful moment for half a second before I stood and went back inside. I wasn't here enjoying a few weeks of vacation; I was here on duty.

Whatever peace I'd achieved sitting outside listening to the night had already been shattered.

I had spent all night awake—and nights on Krozalia were endlessly long. Despite the relaxing ambiance, my eyes had refused to close. Mac had given me some of the local news, even read some of what passed as literature in Krozalia to me. He'd been quiet for the past few hours, however, going about whatever he wished to do when he wasn't witnessing the world through my right eye. And still, the night had gone on. Despite Krozalia being twice the size of Old Earth, the planet's mass was lighter, the gravity-pull lesser, and the days longer. Krozalians compensated by taking four-hour naps every fifteen hours, but I didn't plan to stay long enough to adjust my days accordingly.

I found Vera on the other side of the door with another hovering cart.

"My lady," she said with deference. "I trust you had a relaxing night."

"Yes, thank you," I replied, flustered. I hadn't expected to see her again.

"May I come in?"

I slid to the side without a word, and Vera headed straight to where the sitting area still stood. Aside from moving one of the chairs out to the balcony, I hadn't bothered to return the sitting area to wherever it had come from.

"My lord has requested your presence after you finish your meal," Vera announced as she laid the cart on the table and began to uncover the plates.

"The emperor?" I asked, because I still couldn't understand why the emperor's personal assistant—if that was what Vera really was—was seeing to my needs.

"Yes, my lady."

The food was ordinary human fare: biscuits, cheese, scrambled eggs, and a plate with diced fruits. There was nothing unfamiliar, nothing I'd never tried, and yet, I ate with caution. Vera stayed alert at the edge of the sitting area, hands clasped behind her back, though I thought I heard her muttering once or twice. It was nothing loud enough a human ear could catch, and Mac made no comments, so I let it be.

Once I finished and nothing happened, I let myself relax—until Vera reminded me that the emperor was waiting. She offered to help me do my hair and dress, but I refused. My clothes were clean, fit me well, and let the Kroz know that regardless of my status with the CTF, I was still human. My only concession was to brush my hair, which I then braided, and apply minimal makeup—some eyeliner and lip gloss.

Vera escorted me down several flights of stairs and through several hallways lavishly decorated with statues mounted on pedestals, tapestries, vases, and various gleaming primitive weapons that seemed sharp enough to still be considered lethal.

The further from the wing I'd been staying in, the more Kroz that we encountered. For some reason, I'd expected to be taken to the royal wing and had even looked forward to seeing Dolenta again. But it seemed like Vera was leading me toward the public section of the castle.

"Ask her about where these other hallways go," Mac said. "I want to build a map of the castle to go with the images of the outside."

I opened my mouth to do what he said, but the way Vera was eyeing me made me hold back the questions. It wasn't that her expression made me wary, but rather the lack of one.

"I don't like the way she looks at you when I speak,"

Mac murmured, his voice barely a vibration in my ear.

I had noticed the odd looks, but then again, all Vera's looks were odd. I didn't think she could hear Mac—Baltsar couldn't—but then again, Baltsar was only half Kroz. Maybe his ability was passive while Vera's was active.

I whistled the tune of an old song whose lyrics begged an ex-lover to please go away, never to come calling, never to send gifts again. Mac said nothing to that, which meant he understood I needed him to disengage. Otherwise, he'd have offered a wisecrack.

The further we went, the more Kroz we passed. All were impeccably dressed, with elaborate hairdos and perfect makeup, their jewelry on display. By that point, I expected to find myself in a throne room, filled with guards and courtesans waiting for an audience, but my expectations were wrong again. I was totally blaming all that on Mac and the classics he enjoyed, forcing me to watch and read with him.

The room we entered was guarded by a burly Kroz dressed in armor. He kept his eyes fixed ahead as if he couldn't see or hear Vera and me standing right there.

The room was small compared to the others we had passed, mostly dominated by a large oval table that could sit at least twenty. There was a discreet bar tucked in one corner, a couch in front of an unlit fireplace, and nothing else. No windows to let in the light, no paintings adorned the walls, no rugs softened the dark floor. This was a room where business was conducted, devoid of thrills or distractions.

Emperor Rokoskiv was not alone. No, Ravi was there, seated to his right as they spoke. Both glanced up as we entered—after only a brisk knock—and because my eyes had zeroed in on Ravi, I caught the way he stiffened the moment he saw me. His reaction felt like a blow, but this wasn't the place or time for feelings, so I swallowed my emotions and pulled myself together.

"Captain Leann," the emperor said. "Thank you for coming. Please, have a seat." He indicated the chair to his other side and across from Ravi.

I ventured in cautiously, feeling out of place.

Growing up, my parents had entertained plenty of high-ranking officials, but I'd never been included in any dinner parties. Initially, it was because I was too young to sit with the grownups and later because, as the firstborn, I would never be part of the family business. But I remembered my mother's grace, and despite everything, I was raised with good manners.

"Thank you," I said as I pulled the chair and primly sat.

"Why is she here?" Ravi asked the emperor.

"I invited her."

"Why?" Ravi pressed.

Rather than responding, the emperor turned his gaze behind me. "Vera?"

Before I could turn to look at Vera, Ravi stood, eyes blazing yellow with anger. "Don't," he snapped—at Vera, not the emperor, of course.

I dove off my chair and rolled, coming up in a crouch to face the room. Vera stood behind and to the side of the chair I'd been in, her hands clasped together in front of her. The emperor remained seated but turned to look at me, eyes startled. Embarrassment for overreacting began spreading over my neck and up my face, but I pushed it down. Ravi was the only one who'd moved to the side, but his position only allowed him to see me more clearly. *To attack?* No, to defend, giving the ready position and direction he faced. My discomfiture drained with the realization that maybe I had a reason for alarm. But even that was replaced with resigned caution. I was way in out of my league here.

"What's going on?" I demanded without straightening. I had no chance in hell if any of the Kroz attacked. I would go down, but I wouldn't go down without a fight and plenty of damage. I had known Vera was no ordinary maid, no ordinary Kroz, in fact. I'd been right to suspect her. The only unknown was her exact rank.

"Madrovi. Would you please sit?" The question was

polite, but the look in the emperor's eyes was anything but. "I'll not take offense because I understand the urge to protect can be hard to ignore. But I will not tolerate disrespect." To me, he said, "Please, Captain. We mean you no harm."

I looked at Ravi. I could tell his teeth were clenched even as he obeyed the emperor, but that only made me more nervous. It was the exasperation in the emperor's black eyes that made me straighten—that, and the way he waved at Vera and pointed at the chair at the end of the table. "Sit. I'm tired and the day hasn't even officially started."

Vera sat. After a brief hesitation, so did I.

The emperor didn't waste time diving into the topic. "I was told that you've been genetically enhanced, but that you're not a hypermorph."

I glanced at Ravi, but his expression had completely shut down. For some reason, I'd believed he'd keep my secret.

Foolish me.

"I'm not going to go into an explanation of why hypermorphs are a danger to everyone. But I would be remiss in my duties as a ruler if I let the possibility of a hypermorph go without a thorough examination." He nodded to the end of the table where Vera sat. "I've also decided not to repay the person who brought my daughter home with subterfuge and treachery. It's the reason I asked for your presence for this debriefing. Vera?"

I shifted to look at the Kroz woman, heart pounding like mad in my chest.

"She had a severe reaction to the Comula," Vera began without preamble. "The right side of her body blitzed but didn't shut down. She also remained cognizant and responsive. Her brainwave spikes with low hearing and her reactions are on par with hypermorphs. Her bioelectricity lacks any artifice, however. Her right side is entirely artificial and seems to be adapted for weapons, but all commands originate from the brain and occur naturally. She has the habit of carrying on a one-sided conversation when alone. During such, her cybernetics are more active."

"Meaning?"

"She has some sort of artificial intelligence, but it seems to be for the interactive facilitation of her mechanical parts."

My heart was beating so hard, so loud in my ears, I almost missed the emperor's next words.

"Is she active in stasis?" he asked, casually enough that he might as well have been asking about the weather on some distant planet.

"No. Asleep, her body doesn't respond to stimuli."

It took me five seconds to process the fact that Vera had spied on me when I was sleeping. Which meant she'd been spying on me even before she'd come knocking the first time. Under the table, I clenched my hands to stem their shaking.

"Your assessment?"

Vera considered the question for some time. "She has artificial enhancements that break our law, but she's still human."

The emperor turned to Ravi next.

"Human," Ravi said. Reluctantly, he added, "Her energy pattern is vibrant when she's awake, mute when she's asleep and unconscious."

I lowered my eyes. The stab of betrayal I felt was swift and true, penetrating the haze of panic and piercing the soft muscles of my heart. My nails bit harder into my palms as I gritted my teeth.

"And the others?" the emperor continued, oblivious to my pain. Not that I thought my feelings mattered to him.

"Suffered no reactions whatsoever. The commodore refused the Comula."

The emperor clasped his hands atop the table. There was a platinum wedding band on his pinky finger, the feminine shape—twin to the golden, masculine one on his other hand—told me it belonged to his mate. The emperor studied me with fathomless eyes. "Is the commodore like you, or a hypermorph?"

"No. He just doesn't trust foreign food."

"Does he know about your condition?"

"No."

"Why is he so keen to take you back to the Confederacy?"

I sighed. "Because he's an asshole and he thinks returning me would give him some recognition in the government."

The emperor leaned forward. "Why? Soldiers defect all the time. Why would bringing you back raise his status with the military?"

"I don't know. He knows I don't want to go and he's always been petty like that."

"Captain Leann is the best pilot the Confederacy's ever had," Ravi put in. "After witnessing her in action, I would say she's better than our best too. I can testify to her skills."

That seemed to pique the emperor's interest. "Is it because of her enhancements?"

"She was the best before that," Ravi replied. Damned if he didn't sound so proud. "Her name is at the top for all the best talents—combat, strategy, piloting, among a few others."

"Does anyone in the CTF know about your condition?" the emperor asked me.

"No."

"Lie," Vera said quietly from the other end of the table.

"Excuse me?" I shifted to frown at her, but Ravi spoke before I could.

"Sullivan knows," Ravi interjected. "He found out when Thern injured her."

"Anyone else aside from him?"

"Not that I'm aware."

This time, Vera didn't speak.

"You told Lord Drax that you destroyed the lab and killed the scientists who did this to you. We checked and the facility you mentioned burned down over eight years ago. The records said it was a prosthetic manufacturer. Vera has informed me your entire right side has been altered. Were all your alterations done there?"

"As far as I can remember."

"How many like you were there?"

"I was the only one," I said reluctantly. "There were others brought in, but most never survived the changes done to their bodies, much less progressed to further experiments."

"Do you know who backed the research?"

"No."

"Does your government have any part in it?"

I took a moment to formulate my answer. Ravi shifted at that. The emperor's gaze grew sharper and more focused. I didn't look at Vera when I spoke.

"If there's a person in the human government working for these labs, he or she is not operating with the government's knowledge. As someone facing dissenters, I am sure you understand that there is no such thing as unanimous agreement in any government. If there's a faction out there conducting illegal enhancements, they do not have the human government's knowledge or approval."

It wasn't the most diplomatic answer, but there was no denying that such a faction existed. The point was to make the emperor understand that even if the scientists were human, they were not working for the government. Emperor Rokoskiv was not someone I wanted to aim at the humans.

"What about the HSA?" he asked.

"The Human Supreme Assembly is a large government. They don't directly deal with the CTF or any other divisions in Confederacy Space. They oversee the departments and agencies that are in turn responsible for other departments and agencies on human-inhabited planets and colonies."

The emperor studied me for a few long seconds, his penetrating gaze unnerving. "There are several prosthetic manufacturers in Confederacy Space, but only a handful of them integrate their works with cybernetic control systems. Two were destroyed in the past seven years. Strangely, there were no investigation reports filed in either case, and both incidents were dismissed as accidents."

For once, I was grateful that my heart had been racing since I'd entered the room. I kept my gaze level and innocent. But whatever confession the emperor wanted to hear, he seemed to have read it from my face. A wry smile tugged at one corner of his mouth. "Are there others?" he asked.

Damn it, I wasn't an open book. In fact, I had always been an accomplished liar. "Not that I could find," I replied succinctly. None of the other illegal facilities I destroyed worked with bioengineering and genetic manipulation. Drugs, stolen organs, forbidden artifacts, yes. But aside from the two prosthetic manufactures, I never found a lead back to the scientists.

"We might be able to help each other. If you allow my people to examine the mechanics of your prosthetic limbs, there might be something they can use to track—"

"No," Ravi said, interrupting the emperor. "You told me just a physical. You're not going to take her apart to see how her body functions."

I choked at that, but neither Kroz paid me any attention, too busy staring each other down. I thought for sure the emperor was going to call in his guards and send Ravi to the dungeons. Or punish him for insubordination. He did none of that. Incredibly, the emperor chuckled and waved his hand. "I forgot how obnoxious this bond can be. Very well, just the physical. It'll take more time and work, but I'm sure the labs can identify the patterns needed." He returned his attention to me, but Ravi had yet to relax. "Do you agree?"

"Do I have a choice?" I asked.

"Yes," Ravi asserted before the emperor could answer.

The emperor ignored him. "I don't want to force you," he said honestly. He didn't add "but I will," and he didn't have to. The promise was implied.

"I've already destroyed the manufacturer. I don't think searching for patterns would make a difference, even if you could pinpoint it."

"Have you ever heard about Kukona mineral?"

The abrupt shift in topic made my eye twitch. "It's come up a few times during the journey here."

"Before that."

"No."

Emperor Rokoskiv leaned forward and lowered his voice. "Yet KKM is a component of your prosthetics."

Chapter 9

I blanched. Thoughts and ideas flashed in my head so fast that my mind might as well have been blank.

The emperor leaned back, seemingly satisfied with my reaction. "You really didn't know."

I shook my head.

"Have you ever wondered why Krozalia is so special?" he asked, his non sequitur making me wonder if he was trying to overthrow my mental equilibrium. If so, he was doing an excellent job.

"No."

Emperor Rokoskiv's left eyebrow arched. "It's a common question posed by foreigners on a regular basis. When the Kroz first arrived in Krozalia, we only had passive magic." He cocked his head. "Do you know the difference between passive and active magic?"

"Yes."

"Good. Millennia ago, we were forced to leave our home planet. We came here, an unfamiliar planet that could accommodate the Kroz and hopefully allow us to thrive. The planet ticked all the boxes: abundant landmass, ample water, breathable air, fertile lands teeming with wildlife. It boasted timber, minerals, and a full spectrum of seasons, and it had yet to be conquered. A blank slate, so to speak, for our people to start over.

"I'll not delve into the details, because I don't have all day. In our home planet, KKM existed in meager quantities, a finger here, another there. It grew in deep caves and in very small amounts. One bountiful harvest yielded less than the weight of a newborn. We reserved it for our more advanced technology.

"But once we settled and started charting a detailed map of Krozalia, we discovered that the planet not only grew the KKM but that it had extensive reservoirs with tons and tons of the mineral. Our leaders were not happy. KKM is highly radioactive, and it needs special machines and conditions for harvesting. It was decided that we would protect the site and extract the amount that was necessary—spaceships, medical units, heavy machinery, and no more."

The emperor pressed his index finger on a seemingly empty spot on the table, and at the center, a 3D image of giant purple crystals appeared. I couldn't tell what it was, only that it looked like stalactites from the caves near the cove of my parents' summer cottage. And that it was glowing.

"This is one of our smaller KKM reservoirs," the emperor said.

"I-I have that inside me?" I stammered, horrified. I frowned down at my hand, not sure if I was expecting to see something different than what I saw every day—pale, unblemished skin. Then I shook my head. "I've seen the metal casing of my prosthetic before. It doesn't glow like that. It's not purple—it doesn't glow at all."

The emperor laced his fingers atop the table. "It wouldn't. The KKM acts as an amplifier. Your prosthetics would have anything between ten and thirty grams, no more. Within your body, it augments your endurance, healing, strength, metabolism, cognitive process, and so on. In its natural habitat, KKM intensifies the emission of neon and argon gases native to their location, causing the mineral to glow a purplish hue, enhancing the brilliance of each other until the glare is so bright, you need special goggles to prevent blindness. It becomes ripe for mining when it develops a hard shell. It's this shell that we harvest, not the glowing crystal.

"It takes between ten and fifty years for the shell to develop, and a day's work to harvest one shell. However, if the

KKM isn't mined, the planet's density increases, and the entire geological and ecological cycles are disrupted."

Realization hit me then. "You have to mine the KKM whether you want it or not."

"Yes. Luckily for us, the KKM is very useful. But it's also dangerous, and we carefully assess who we sell it to."

My eyes bulged. "You think whoever is funding the scientists, that they have someone here in Krozalia too?"

The pained look in the emperor's eyes prompted me to reconsider my line of thought.

"No, you think that a Kroz is backing the scientists." The idea sounded ludicrous, and I thought the emperor would laugh it up. He didn't.

"There are only a handful of feasible scenarios, each one more improbable than the other. Yet, KKM is native to Krozalia. There's no longer any planet anywhere in the known galaxy where the mineral can be mined. Allowing my people to examine you will help us narrow down which mine yours came from, and from there, it's only a matter of going over the logs. Who has clearance, who was working the mines, who packed them up, and more importantly, we'll be able to cross-reference them with the prosthetic manufacturers."

I doubted it would be that straightforward.

Ravi stood and the emperor looked at him. "It's not a threat we can allow to grow. The CTF is aware of this. We might even be able to trace the harvest spot if we can detect traces of the tools used in the manufacturing." He switched to Krozalian and continued on.

Guilt and resignation crossed Ravi's expression. He said one word and exited the room after he cast a brief glance my way.

We watched him go, Vera implacably, the emperor with some sympathy. "I apologize for Madrovi's primitive behavior," he said conciliatorily. "It's not easy to stand aside and do nothing as our life-mates face hardship."

I didn't correct his assumption about my relationship with

Ravi. His misconception could very well have been the reason for his civility and I saw no reason to rectify that. Then something the emperor said occurred to me. "What did you mean when you said that the CTF is aware of this?"

The emperor was quiet for several moments, regarding me as his fingertips tapped on the tabletop. "We've always disregarded humans from previous inquiries as the least likely culprits whenever we apprehended genetically enhanced individuals. Yes, human had the knowledge to create androids and lifelike AIs, but we never believed them capable of creating hypermorphs."

"Because Kukona mineral is the key," I breathed. He had said as much in his explanation; I just hadn't connected the dots until then.

"Yes."

"I see."

"Do you? You think it's a coincidence that the Confederacy is asking to sign a trade agreement for the Kukona mineral at this time?"

I began to defend the CTF and then stopped. I had considered that the moment he'd mentioned it being present in my body, but had dismissed it just as fast. Why? Because if they knew that Kukona mineral was an essential component to create hypermorphs, they wouldn't approach the Kroz in an official capacity.

"You think they would have proposed the agreement if they intended to use it to break the law?" I countered.

The emperor inclined his head. "Sometimes, people won't suspect foul play when the other person is acting in broad view. Eleven years ago, we caught wind of a potential hypermorph lab that we tracked down to the edges of Confederacy Space. The Kroz are the overseers of the hypermorph's ban, but we don't condone the overstepping of our authority. We granted the CTF the opportunity to investigate and either deal with the lab or request aid. When my people asked for a status report, they presented us with what I believe now were fictitious documents and called it a false alarm."

He fell silent at that, expression expectant.

I licked my lips and wiped my suddenly clammy hands on the linen of my pants. "The Genesis Mission?" I guessed, my thoughts going straight to Alex. I was aware of Vera's heavy gaze on me, but I didn't take my attention off the emperor.

"Yes. Was that where you were taken from?"

I dipped my chin. "Does the CTF forward you the details for missions? Archives, the hypermorphs they capture?" I thought my voice was casual, but Emperor Rokoskiv's gaze was shrewd. In the very back of my mind, I understood I might have said something wrong, but if I did, I still needed to know. I needed to know if Alex had ever been sent here or if his body was ever found. The files I'd taken from the dark lab were meticulous, listing the names and dates for each individual they'd experimented on—the dates they were brought in, in what state they were, dates of birth, social status, medical conditions, and race. They also listed each experiment tried, the subject's reaction and the effect of the experiment. Alex's name was there, his status listed as inconclusive, but nothing else. No date of relocation, failure, or death.

"There are several laws passed galaxy-wide," the emperor was saying. "Not all of them are overseen by the Kroz. Hypermorphs fall under our jurisdiction because when it comes down to it, we have more experience. So, yes, any rumors, investigations, sightings, and anything pertaining to hypermorphs are brought to our attention. In instances where an opposing faction governs the area, we offer them a timeframe to investigate and terminate the threat, or give the option of assistance. If they fail, then we step in and wrest control of the situation.

"But to answer your question, we haven't caught a hypermorph for over two decades, the last of which self-terminated before we could question its making. Since then, we've caught genetically enhanced individuals, but never someone as close to being a hypermorph as you."

Imperial Stardust

That meant the public executions that the Kroz broadcast every year were... "Genetically enhanced individuals, nothing more," the emperor said, and I glanced sharply at him.

"The thought was clear on your face," he said with a half-smile reminiscent of Dolenta's. "We're willing to overlook what you are on the account this was done against your will and your actions to date. In exchange, I'm asking for your full cooperation to help us solve this problem."

"I don't know who's behind the research and where they are. I'd have gone after them if I did."

The emperor nodded, a look of understanding in the cold black of his eyes. "The combination of genetic manipulation and AIs is banned for a reason. Not all hypermorphs are created the same way, but genetic manipulation with KKM always result in a hypermorph. It's why the ban is in place. We can control who we sell the KKM to, but once it's out of our hands, all we can do is make sure that the punishment for breaking the law is swift and harsh."

And here the CTF was, trying to start a trade agreement for the mineral. Sullivan's words from a few days ago on the *Splendor* came back to mind: "There were three of them. They were all Cradoxian teenagers. Kids who were born and raised on the Inner Planets. Clara...Leann...They were all hypermorphs."

I knew why the CTF wanted the KKM: they had just discovered the hypermorphs' secret ingredient. But what did they plan to do with it? Create their own army? Build weapons effective against the Kukona mineral? Use it to conquer Cradoxian Space?

I rubbed the palms of my hands over my face. I was aware of both Emperor Rokoskiv and Vera's eyes on me. Here wasn't the place to get lost in my thoughts.

"When do you want me to have this physical done and where?"

"We have an execution in the afternoon, and a farewell ceremony tomorrow for the warriors who fell with the *Wedva-Xa*. Vera can escort you after that."

"All right."

The door opened and Ravi walked in. I could make out Zafra leaning against the wall outside before he shut it again and stalked to the seat across from mine.

"Can I ask for a favor in return?" I asked the emperor. Ravi stiffened, but I ignored him.

The emperor tilted his head as if the idea of someone asking him for something was a foreign concept. "Yes?"

"I know you distrust the CTF and the convenient timing for the trade request. But is it possible to have someone at least hear the commodore out? I'm not asking you to agree," I hastened to add when the emperor's expression turned thunderous. "I understand, given the current situation, you'd be inclined to reject them, but all I ask is that you listen to their proposal before declining, nothing more." And I was going to have a long talk with Lorenzo. If they wanted the KKM, they'd better have a plausible reason for it. And they'd better come clean with the Kroz.

A few tense seconds went by. I was afraid to hold the emperor's gaze, but I also didn't want to look away. I fixed my eyes on his chin and waited.

"We'll hear them out," the emperor finally said. He leaned forward, depthless eyes meeting and holding mine. "But I will hold you accountable if they lie or try to manipulate the talks to their benefit."

I suppressed a grimace and told myself it was what I got for playing politics.

"You're dismissed."

I practically jumped off my seat in my hurry.

"Captain Leann?"

I turned back. "Yes?"

"The princess seems to have formed an attachment to you and has asked for permission to visit." The bafflement in his eyes told me he couldn't see what a Kroz child found interesting in a human captain, but it was more genuine curiosity than an insult.

I smiled. "I'd love that."

Emperor Rokoskiv motioned with a hand. "It's settled then."

Vera stood, and my stomach quivered with anxiety.

"Stay," Ravi told her. "Zafra and Furox will escort the captain."

Vera waited for the emperor to nod before resuming her seat. I wasn't sure if switching Vera for Zafra was much improvement, but it wasn't like I had any say in it.

Chapter 10

There was a tall Kroz with spiky blood-red hair leaning against the wall across from Zafra. Both had on Kroz armor, but I didn't remember seeing him before.

"You seem none the worse for wear," Zafra observed, gracefully pushing away from the wall and falling in step beside me.

I tilted my head to the side. "Should I have?"

The other Kroz snorted. "People who usually spend time with those three either leave in tears or in a body bag." He extended a hand to me. "We didn't get introduced before. Name is Furox, First Division, Third Battalion."

I shook the offered hand and eyed him. "What does the ranking mean?"

Zafra snickered. "That he's a moron and a braggart."

"It means I'm in the first division and third squad battalion."

I nodded sagely and Zafra laughed out loud. It was a nice laugh, the kind that compelled you to laugh along.

"Shut up," Furox muttered, but a smile tugged at the corners of his lips. "You don't want to bruise my ego."

We turned a corner and came face-to-face with two tall Kroz, a woman and a man in their mid-to-late thirties. We halted in front of them. Chills skated down my spine, triggered by the hawkish intensity in the woman's gaze.

She studied me as if I were a specimen under a microscope, looking me up and down as if searching for something.

"Vroja Lorvel," Furox said, closing the gap and bending

to kiss her on each cheek. He said something in Krozalian that sounded complimentary, then turned to the other Kroz and shook his hand. "Vroj Ozvie."

On the right side of my vision, words appeared.

Vroja: Aunt. Vroj: Uncle.

I clasped my hands behind my back and listened to the exchange of Krozalian pleasantries. Mac didn't translate again or say anything, which I guessed meant the conversation wasn't relevant. Since we had left Vera and her intrusive magic and he hadn't burned my eardrum with his assessment of the meeting I'd just escaped, whatever he was doing, he was too busy to spare me more than a few words. It wasn't something uncommon, but rather that the emperor's words had instigated a line of inquiry he wanted to pursue. Hopefully, he wouldn't find himself so curious as to disregard my warning not to go hacking again.

I brought my attention back to the two strange Kroz and wondered if it was polite to excuse myself. I needed to talk to Lorenzo and discuss the KKM deal. If the CTF had a plausible reason to request a trade, their best course of action would be disclosing it to the Kroz and appealing to them. I waited for the lull of Furox's rapid-fire Krozalian so I could excuse myself.

Ozvie was taller than Furox but just as broad. He had a tan complexion, dark hair, and he reminded me a bit of Ravi with his chiseled jaw and umber eyes.

Zafra cut off Furox with an exasperated hand wave. "Mada," she said to the Kroz woman, then switched to Universal, assumedly for my benefit. "What are you doing here? I thought you didn't have any businesses in the city until next week." Mada—I knew that term even before Mac translated it for me. It meant mother in Krozalian. I glanced between the two, searching for the resemblance. It was there, but not in a mother-daughter likeness, more like sister-to-sister ones.

The woman's eyes—as green as Zafra's now that I was looking—shifted away from me, where they had been focused for the most part since we'd turned the corner.

"There was a call for a meeting," she answered in lilting Universal. She turned back to me and extended a hand. "I'm Lorvel."

I took the hand and shook it once. "Leann."

"This is my mate, Ozvie."

"It is nice to meet you, Lady Leann," Ozvie said and extended his hand.

I took it. He had the hands of someone who enjoyed physical labor: calloused and rough.

Lorvel drew closer. I forced myself to stay still and not flinch, even though every part of my being wanted me to step back and away.

"You're the captain Madrovi brought home, the human that everyone is talking about." From the way her mouth tilted at the corners, that "talk" seemed to amuse her now that she'd seen me. Oddly enough, there wasn't any disgust or hostility in her expression, just humor. I wasn't sure if it was a good thing or not.

"I guess I am?" I said, but it came out as a question.

Lorvel smiled and turned to Zafra, her interest in my presence gone. "You're going out?"

The loss of her attention made me breathe easier, as if her gaze had been a fixed weight on my chest.

Zafra dipped her chin. "For a while."

Lorvel shifted and touched a hand to the elbow of the Kroz beside her. "We'll let you go then. I have someone I need to see before the meeting."

We stepped aside and they moved passed us and around the corner.

Beside me, Furox was grinning from ear to ear, eyes dancing with mirth. "Do you think I can sneak in behind them?"

"No," Zafra snapped. To me, she said, "Ignore him." And motioned for us to continue.

We emerged onto a small balcony at the next corner. It overlooked the front foyer of the castle. Tall, double doors allowed the natural light to flood in and framed a picturesque view of blooming, multicolored flowers.

"I'll choose the destination as recompense for my bruised ego," Furox announced, alluding to the conversation that meeting his aunt and uncle had interrupted.

"Your ego can't be bruised," Zafra scoffed. "It's as hard as your head."

"Destination?" I repeated.

Zafra turned to me. "Ravi suggested we take you sightseeing."

I stopped walking. "You don't have to do that," I said.

"Oh, come on," Mac protested. "I'd like to see Krozalia too. Just because you command the body doesn't mean you get to make all the decisions."

"Of course we do," Furox said. "It's not every day that my commander orders me to drop my duties and entertain guests. Come on, I know the perfect spot to take you."

Zafra groaned. "Please, not the Flying Crown."

"You can stay behind," Furox sniffed. "I'm perfectly capable of showing the captain around on my own." He threw one arm around my shoulder and guided me down the stairs.

"Please, you'll be too busy flirting with your mate to order a drink, much less entertain a guest."

"I can multitask," Furox said. "Besides, a man has needs. I have to see my woman and son now and again."

"You saw her when you took her to work less than two hours ago."

"And now I can see her again." He turned to me and gave me sad puppy eyes. "Unless you object?"

I chuckled. "Not at all."

"No, no." Zafra waved her hands in the air as if to erase Furox's words. "We'll give her a tour of the capital." She glared at Furox, silencing his protest. "We'll take her on a tour, and then we'll go to the Flying Crown."

"I agree," Mac said. "Now, please say yes."

"Okay. Tour first," I said, more to appease Mac than the two Kroz glaring at each other.

"Fine," Furox grumbled. "But if my woman leaves me because she doesn't see enough of me, I'll blame the two of you."

"Your woman will thank us for keeping you from underfoot," Zafra retorted.

Furox gasped in mock horror. "She would never. My mate loves me so much that she eagerly awaits my return, constantly checking the time and her commlink for word of my arrival."

"Whatever. Save it for someone who cares."

Chapter 11

Lord Drax

My mother finished paying her respects to the emperor and turned on me. "Madrovi Fidraxi," she snapped, her voice cracking like the lash of a whip. "What is this I hear that you've claimed a human?"

"Hello, mother," I said and kissed both her cheeks. "It's good to see you."

Her eyes softened and she touched her palm to my cheek. "I'm glad you returned safely, and am sorry for the loss of your crew."

"Thank you."

"Now, explain to me why I only heard of the claim when I reached the city, and from Xoda of all people!"

I winced. I'd known word would travel fast and that I'd need to contact my parents, but I'd figured I'd have at least three days. Still, I knew my mother was more hurt that she heard about it through her nemesis than she was angry at me. I brought her hand to my mouth, then pressed it against my forehead in apology. "I am deeply sorry, Mada. I had a lot on my mind. I wasn't thinking."

She huffed, appeased but clearly still peeved. "I don't understand how Xoda, of all people, would learn about it before I did."

"I claimed her in front of my cadre," I confessed. Tregoe was Xoda's son and a member of Zafra's squad. He'd have passed on the news the moment he was relieved from duty. "If it helps, she's my mate-match."

My mother sniffed, but I saw the glint of delight in her

eyes. The news pleased her, as I knew it would.

"Would you have brought her home to introduce us if I hadn't come?"

I paused before answering. Not because I didn't want to, but because things here were too volatile and I didn't know how things would unfold after the execution.

My hesitation was a mistake. Big mistake. My mother's eyes narrowed. In my peripheral vision, I saw my father grimace and edge closer to the emperor.

"You weren't going to, were you? You planned to mate a human, forgo the celebrations, and what? Call me when your first child was born?"

A thrill of anticipation ran down my sternum at the thought of a child, but I clamped it down. "It's not like that," I began.

"It's good then that I met her on my way in and took her measure."

"You did?" I asked, looking up at my father for some indication of how the meeting went.

"Yes. She's short and a bit on the thin side, but regular meals and a bit of training will build some muscles and definition."

I opened my mouth, then wisely shut it again. "Come, Mother. Let's sit. We can discuss this later, after the meeting with the advisors. We have a lot to discuss and not enough time. We caught a traitor, and things aren't looking good."

My mother's demeanor changed, the careful façade of a warrior replacing the exasperation and love of a few moments ago.

She turned to my father. "I told you it was bad."

"Yes, you did," he agreed, thumping me on the back as he headed for the table.

"Tell us," she demanded as we all took our seats.

Before I'd assumed the position of Head Guard, my father had filled that seat, with my mother one step below. My parents were also close friends with the emperor, maybe the only ones I could, at the moment, vouch for.

I started my explanation with the details of the attack on the *Wedva-Xa*. We were halfway through what had happened when there was a thump at the door. Like a heavy body being thrown against it.

At once, Vera and I were in front of the emperor, with my parents taking pose to either side of the room. A moment later, the doors opened and in walked Linsky, a dark scowl on his face.

"What's going on?" he demanded, searching our defensive posture. Outside, the guard posted by the door was on the ground, either dead or unconscious.

"What did you do to Renzo?" my father demanded, moving past Linsky and kneeling by his body.

"He told me I wasn't allowed in."

The emperor nudged me aside. "Did you have to hit him?" he asked, looking exasperated. It was a stark contrast to the wrath from yesterday, when we were planning how to spy on Linsky and Zefron. "If you haven't heard, there was an attempt on my daughter's life."

"I heard," Linsky said, his concern looking genuine as he approached and placed a hand on the emperor's shoulder. I gnashed my teeth and tried not to react to the threat. Linsky was a traitor and an exceptional liar for having fooled us so thoroughly, but he wasn't foolish. He knew every single person in this room was loyal to the emperor, and any move he made now would be met with deadly force.

On my left, Vera's face was impassive, her posture relaxed. But I knew her well enough to see the homicidal telltale in the contours of her eyes and lips.

"I came to check on you," Linsky was saying. "But the guard outside told me I wasn't allowed in. I was afraid something was going on." He looked back at my father. "I only shocked him unconscious. He should be up in a few minutes. Traux will stand guard until he awakens."

Traux, Linsky's guard, saluted and pulled the door shut, presumably to stand guard outside. Without waiting for a response, Linsky pulled the chair to the emperor's left and sat. "Now, tell me, what happened? I heard you caught a traitor?" he asked me.

"I did. Several traitors, actually," I replied, wanting nothing more than to sunder his lying, duplicitous face from existence. But the emperor wanted Linsky to think he'd dodged discovery, and so I did nothing.

I waited for the emperor to resume his seat to do the same. And then I told Linsky what the emperor told me to say.

"I think I spotted this human captain," Linsky said when I finished. He sat now, relaxed, humor gleaming in his golden eyes. "I heard you claimed her when you arrived. Maybe your distraction allowed the defector to make his move. If you'd been thinking clearly, you might have seen his treachery coming."

Rage, white and hot, spread through my body. I lowered my head in meek submission, hands clenching on my lap.

"Now, Linsky, we all know that's not true," my father interjected. "Ravi earned his position through his own merit."

Linsky's expression turned contrite. "I meant no offense, but maybe a temporary Head of Guard replacement would be prudent. At least until Madrovi is past the claiming stage, or this rebellion nonsense blows over. For your own safety. I have a few trustworthy and competent warriors I can recommend who would be suitable for the task."

"It's all fine, Linsky," the emperor interjected. "We have everything handled. We've already apprehended everyone involved. Execution will take place this afternoon."

Linsky paused at that, something fleeting crossing his expression. "Who else was involved? Please don't tell me there were more royal warriors. Is that why you put someone new at the door?"

"There were four warriors, as well as a few tribesmen."

Linsky jumped to his feet, and Vera and I tensed. My parents just watched the exchange, aware there was an underlying context and unable to identify the threat for what it was. I hadn't told them the part about Linsky and Zefron being part of the coup.

"We need to tighten security in the castle," Linsky announced and pulled out his commlink. "I'll put in a call for standby guards to respond to duty at once, then when the advisors arrive, we'll discuss strategic points."

I gritted my teeth but said nothing. Before the empress had died, such presumptuous behavior would have incurred harsh punishment, but the emperor had granted Linsky too much leeway in the past three years. A glance at the frigid fury in the emperor's eyes told me those days were over. Linsky just didn't know that yet.

And suddenly, I approved the emperor's plan to allow Linsky and his cohorts to believe that they had avoided being caught. I leaned back in my seat and listened to Linsky give the orders I should be giving, and arranging schedules that the emperor should be arranging. Maybe Linsky would be the downfall of his allies after all.

Chapter 12

Krozalia was a planet of wonders and improbabilities. We flew in a luxuriously comfortable hovercraft above large trees, losing sight of the castle behind the canopies within a few minutes, only to reveal the distant telltale of the largest megalopolis I'd ever seen in person.

Skyscrapers spiraled high into the air, like the spears of the victorious after a battle. Hovercrafts of all shapes and sizes zipped between towers like little insects. Bridges, seemingly endless, crisscrossed the cityscape. The closer we ventured, the more intricate the details became, and neither Zafra nor Furox made any comments while I stared out the panoramic windows, gawking like a farmer who'd happened into the city for the first time.

This was Cordolis, Krozalia's capital and the jewel of the empire. It was a busy megalopolis, bustling with life—a riot of diversity, cacophony, and vivid colors. Holographic advertisements painted entire skylines while vendors filled sidewalks and every street corner teemed with activity. Kroz were everywhere, weaving through the urban tapestry.

We circled the city for some time, sometimes on the ground between colossal buildings and other times in the air when traffic on the streets was congested.

Zafra and Furox let me goggle without a word, but when I showed interest in the history of landmarks, they started pointing out things and explaining, taking turns, and adding personal experiences.

"What're all those things attached to that bridge?" I asked, pointing at a bridge so long, the end was lost to distance and mist. What prompted the question though was all the cables protruding from the sides and bottom to disappear under the water like tentacles. I could see the support beams, so I didn't understand what the function of all the extras was for.

"They're the support for Endoy—air, gas, electricity, and all other amenities," Furox explained.

I glanced over, but it was Zafra who answered my next question. "Endoy is an underwater city. It's the biggest we have in Krozalia. Our population has grown exponentially in the last few centuries. So much so that we no longer have enough landmass to house everyone."

"We might be the biggest planet in the galaxy," Furox broke in, "but we're the only habitable one. Besides, there are places on the planet that can never support any life forms."

"The North-West, South-East, and both poles are mainly made up of gases," Zafra said, adding to the explanation. "It's the reason our gravity isn't stronger than it is, considering Krozalia's size."

"Hmm," Mac said. "Do you think these are the locations for the KKM reservoirs? The emperor mentioned neon and argon gases being essential for the KKM's growth. And he did say that if they don't harvest the mineral, the planet's density changes. That would cause heavier gravity and disturb the entire ecosystem."

I agreed. I hadn't known Krozalia had underwater cities, but there was a lot I hadn't known.

"Can we visit Endoy?" I asked, surprised at how much I'd love to see it.

"Not today," Furox said apologetically and thumped the seat beside him. "This baby isn't insulated for underwater foraging."

"Too bad," I murmured, letting the disappointment wash over me. "Where does that bridge go?"

"Sarkar," Zafra answered. "It's the second largest city in Krozalia. It's exotically artistic. If you nag my brother enough, he'll take you there."

My head snapped around. I found her eyes steady on mine. "Brother?"

Furox snorted. "The family resemblance should have given it away. We're all cursed with it."

I looked between the two. I was certain Furox had referred to Lorvel as aunt, while Zafra had called her mother. Maybe Mac was right and his translator was wonky.

No doubt seeing the question in my eyes, Furox explained, "She means Ravi."

My mind blanked a few long seconds before some puzzle pieces fell into place. I turned to Zafra next. "You're both related to Ravi?"

I could believe Furox and Zafra were related to each other—they both had the same complexion and hair coloring—but Ravi's hair was black, his eyes an umber shade, his skin tone darker. More like Ozvie. I made a strangled sound in my throat. "Brother," I whispered.

Misunderstanding my panic, Furox grabbed his chest and mock-shuddered. "No, please. I'm unfortunate enough to be a cousin. She's the one cursed as the baby sister."

I glanced at Zafra. She looked nothing like Ravi, but Ozvie…there had been a resemblance there, in the umber eyes and the powerful jaw.

Oh, good grief. "She—they were his parents?"

Zafra smiled. There was sympathy in her eyes as she gave a single nod.

The uncomfortable feeling that had been present inside me since I'd laid eyes on her unclenched, and I realized that somewhere in my heart, I'd considered this woman competition. Which was ridiculous, all things considered. Sooner or later, I'd leave and Ravi would stay. His life was here and mine…wasn't. A fierce pang of loss made my breath hitch imperceptibly. I wanted that man, his companionship, his thoughtfulness. But I knew I couldn't have him. Maybe in a few years, once I'd done what I needed to do, but not now. It would be foolish, selfish even, to try to start something with him knowing that it would only be for a time. The realization didn't ease the yearning inside me.

Suddenly, both Furox and Zafra jerked upright, almost in perfect unison, and pulled out their commlinks.

"What is it?" I asked, fully alert.

Furox grunted and pressed something on his commlink, and text appeared in front of him. Unfortunately, I could no more read Krozalian than I could speak it. But the holograph image that appeared next, I understood.

A multitude of people congregated like ants in front of a tall spire, waving banners and shouting something that didn't come through the silent holographic vid.

Zafra spewed Krozalian in rapid fire and Furox shifted the view to another angle.

"They're…rioting?" I guessed, unsure exactly of what that scenario meant. I'd seen humans protesting laws and treatments, and even the Conscription Enforcement Act a time or two, but here in Krozalia, for all I knew, they could be celebrating.

"Something like that," Furox said, zooming the images in and out so fast, my stomach roiled with vertigo.

I looked at Zafra doing the same with her images, and then out the window.

"Mac? What's going on?" I asked.

We were hovering above an expansive rooftop park, filled with trees, people, and recreational equipment.

"Seems like the Kroz are demanding answers from the emperor," Mac said. "I can't find much, only that that they want the transparency they're due. Give me a few minutes and I'll see what I can find."

"Here." Zafra pointed to a tower that resembled a crowned wand.

"The university?" Furox asked, moving the holograph image around and studying it from all sides. "You're sure?"

"It'll be easier for containment," she said.

Furox did something on his commlink. The hovercraft

did a one-eighty spin and sped away like a missile. In the holograph, a red dot approached the building Zafra had pointed to, and given the similar building zooming outside the window, it was obvious we were the red dot.

"I'm sorry," Zafra told me as she pulled a large box from under her seat. "We'll have to postpone breakfast."

"It's fine," I said. "I ate before I met with the emperor. How can I help?"

Zafra glanced up at me. "You stay put. Reinforcements will be here soon. We're simply going to contain the mob until they arrive."

"Contain *how*? There were literally thousands in that group." And only two of you, I added silently.

Furox smiled faintly. "There's a reason the royal warriors are both feared and respected."

"And that is?"

"We're each worth a thousand Kroz."

He wasn't bragging, just stating a fact. Shivers went down my spine at the eager look in his eyes. He was going to enjoy this.

"It just looks like people decided to group and go shout in that spot for no apparent reason," Mac told me. "I can't find anything on the instigators, and from the satellite view, there isn't much to see."

"What's so special about their chosen location?" I asked, deciding the less Mac searched, the less likely he'd be tempted to do something that would come back to bite me in the ass.

"That's the Garden Ministry," Zafra said, rummaging inside the box, which was filled with various weapons. "The advisors have an open room for the public there. It's where complaints are received, grants are given, renovation plans are made, and so on."

She was laying down weapons as she spoke—a laser pistol, a long-range stunner, a small disk that seemed to swallow the light, a ruby red pouch that she opened, looked inside, and placed beside the laser pistol.

Imperial Stardust

Furox finished pressing on his commlink and gave a one-word command in Krozalian. The tip of the spiral surrounding the crowned wand rotated outward, revealing a flat expense that could fit the *Splendor* comfortably. The tip began shifting, unfolding like a compass needle and extending as the joints snapped together. They attached to the side of the spiral like railway tracks, and I couldn't understand what was going on until the hovercraft lowered to the start of the tracks on the flat expense. Something clamped the undercarriage of the hovercraft and the snap-snap-snap reverberated through the cabin.

Furox lowered his commlink and looked at me. "Brace yourself," he said just as the seat underneath me shifted.

Harnesses went around my shoulders and strapped me in. The same happened to Zafra and Furox, though both seemed unimpressed.

The next moment, we were hurtling down the side of the spiral so fast the images outside the window were nothing more than a blur of various colors. The entire descent went by in five seconds flat.

Over two hundred floors and five seconds later, the carriage was cruising into the street adjacent to the protesting crowd. Furox pressed a button on the side of the carriage and a window opened. With that one motion, the world came alive around us. Shouting and hot air and smells invaded the cab of the hovercraft, so much at once that it took me a dazed moment to adjust to the sensory onslaught.

Furox and Zafra were already stepping out, their armor shifting and growing over their necks, covering the backs of their heads and faces. By the time it was done, two unidentifiable Kroz warriors stood in front of me.

"Please stay put," Furox said as Zafra rushed toward the crowd. "Reinforcements will be here soon." Without waiting for my reply, he rushed after Zafra.

"Are you going to stay?" Mac asked.

I glanced back into the hovercraft, but the box with the weapons was tucked back in place. I didn't think it was unlocked, and a tug proved me right. I grunted, shut the door, and hurried after the two Kroz.

"I didn't think you would," Mac said. "There are some kind of law enforcement personnel already trying to break the crowd and keep damages at a minimum, but they're not making much headway."

"I don't understand. What does protesting in that spot accomplish?"

"I don't know. Their formation looks bizarre to me, though it could be the overhead angle."

"Great, my AI thinks people are bizarre."

"Admit it. If people wanted to protest some injustice, they should have marched to the palace."

"Maybe they can't?" I hit the side street and followed the increasing commotion and shouts. "What are they saying?"

"The roads to the palace are open, and I don't know. It's some sort of war hymn that I can't find a translation for."

I reached the large avenue and came to a stop. Ahead, a wall of Kroz blocked my path, but it wasn't like I knew where to go. There was barely a fist of space between one person and the next, yet, it seemed almost…orderly? As if there had been thought and organization behind it. "I get what you mean," I remarked, looking around.

Zafra and Furox were nowhere to be seen. There was a squat cart a bit behind and I sprinted that way, belatedly realizing there was a woman beside it. I climbed atop it and turned to look.

Rows and rows of Kroz stood, shouting in perfect harmony. It was as if an invisible conductor had orchestrated their stances with a giant ruler.

"Mw tan Kol!" they called. "Tan miha vol!"

There was another phrase I couldn't make out, not as loud or as clear as the others. "Bizarre indeed," I murmured, jumping off the cart before the Kroz woman could swat my legs with a baton she'd pulled from a drawer on the side of the cart. "This looks spontaneous, but it's too organized to be so."

"Maybe the Kroz are naturally that organized," Mac

speculated.

"I don't think so," I said. "I'll believe they live an organized life, but what they're doing here takes rehearsal. Whatever this is, they've practiced for it. What else can you see from above?"

"Three of the Kroz began moving away from your friends the moment they appeared. One is going in the direction of the university building, the other just entered the blue spire, and the third will appear about a hundred meters to your left if she doesn't change trajectory."

"All right," I said, veering to the left. "What's suspicious about them?"

"For starters, they're carrying weapons and moving against the crowd," Mac said. "And I recognized the Kroz who went into the blue spire. He was in Zafra's crew at the spaceport."

"Which one?"

"Evo. The one with the scalp tattoo."

"He could be here to help, same as Furox and Zafra."

"Could be, but the moment the three spotted armored warriors, they broke apart and hurried away."

I looked up at the blue spire. The surface was made of blue glass that simulated ocean waves gleaming under the sun.

"Two military convoys are approaching the building where you parked. They should reach the crowd in the next few minutes."

I grunted. "What's that building?"

"A shopping plaza. You should take Cassandra there."

"Do you have eyes inside?"

"Depends why you're asking," Mac replied innocently. "If you're worried I might trigger an alarm piggybacking into their security feed, then I don't. If you're asking because you want to know where Evo is going, then yes, and he's just entered a room on the fifth floor."

"Damn it, Mac."

"Don't," he said. "It's a shopping plaza, unassociated

with the Kroz government, and there's nothing to tie me or the *Splendor* should their security discover an intruder."

"Fine. Which one is the fifth floor?" I glanced up the building façade and Mac marked a red X on said floor on my right vision.

"What's in the room?" I asked.

"Can't find any systems to hack in, but from the schematics, it should look down at the front of the building."

A Kroz woman broke from the crowd a few meters to my left and hurried through the loosely gathered onlookers, then crossed the street, heading this way.

"I bet you ten universals that she's going to go into the building behind you and climb to the fifth or sixth floor."

I glanced at the building behind me, then at the blue spire, then further on to the crowned university building. "Do you have eyes on those buildings too?"

I had once watched a movie where a gang of fifty had been ambushed by three thugs who'd been hiding in surrounding trees. They'd formed an equilateral triangle, and when the gang had reached the midpoint, the three had attacked with laser guns. Hidden in the trees, by the time the gang figured out where the shots were coming from, most lay dead or wounded. I had a feeling this tactic was being put to use now.

"Do you want me to?"

"Mac," I snapped.

"So bossy," he muttered. "No, I haven't breached their defenses, yet. Their firewall systems are more robust and sophisticated than those of the shopping plaza."

"Let me know the moment you do."

"Sure."

"This does not mean you can hack the palace," I warned.

"Mmm-hmm," he said. "Six Kroz warriors have joined the melee. They're all in full armor, so I can't discern who is who, but I bet Ravi is among them."

"Keep me updated," I said and looked back at the woman. "Do you recognize her?"

"No."

I wondered if she was some sort of assassin, black ops, or spy. But who was her target? Zafra, Furox, the royal warriors in general? Or maybe the advisors? The crowd was, after all, protesting in front of their building. I had a feeling though the mayhem was just the distraction.

I hesitated on the street, then pivoted and went after the woman. "Send a text to Ravi about those three, tell him I think the people are a diversion."

I'd just finished telling Mac that when there was a loud crack and I spun, hands up in defense. I hadn't grasped how annoying all that shouting had been until the sound had cut off. Not only that but every single person I could see was frozen in place, their arms still raised, mouths open.

"Ah, I see," Mac said. "Two of the royal warriors have some kind of energy damper—some sort of crowd control magic. I bet it's one of the devices Zafra packed when she grabbed that box."

I recalled the black disk and the pouch. They were the only two things I wasn't familiar with. "Nifty," I said.

"Sure. But that only made the Kroz warriors stand out as they move about the paralyzed people."

"They're the target," I said with certainty and ran for the building the woman had entered. "Text Ravi that."

"He just sent you one telling you to get back to the hovercraft. I think he's under the illusion that you take orders from him."

"Just send him that warning," I huffed under my breath.

"Sure. There. I even added a few kissing graphs."

I let out a frustrated growl, but it wasn't like I could do anything about it now. *Hey, Ravi, ignore the kisses. They're not from me; they're from my AI.*

The lobby of the building was a wide, open area adorned with potted trees and sculpted pillars. Pastel paintings decorated some of the walls. At the far end, large glass doors overlooked a garden. I spotted the Kroz just as she was disappearing behind one of the sculptures and sprinted that way, my footsteps echoing heavily.

Something came flying at my head the moment I turned the corner. I threw myself to the left, rolled back, and scrambled to my feet.

"Watch it!" Mac screeched. "That's a Shivarhi Blade."

Oh good, a blade that could cut steel. I dodged another slice to the shoulder, but not the next. Instead of pulling away, I dove for the Kroz. It was a reckless move, or an ingenious one, depending on who you asked. The predictable thing would have been to keep dodging until I got sliced to pieces, but death by a thousand cuts was not on my agenda. I preferred my body in one piece, thank you very much. Or as much of one as I could keep, considering some of my limbs were mechanical already.

I hit the woman dead center and we both went down hard. Before I'd been captured by the scientists, I weighed about fifty-some kilos. After they finished replacing my right side with wires and metal, my weight tripled. The scientists had that one thing going for them: they knew what they were doing. Had my artificial limbs not been programmed to respond to brain signals to lift and lower upon command, my shoulders and hips would have dislocated at best, broken off and fallen at worst. Unfortunately, even though the Kroz woman wheezed when we fell, her grip on the blade didn't loosen. I seized her hand and clamped her wrist, pressing on the nerves and slamming it repeatedly against the hard tile.

The woman snapped something in Krozalian that sounded nasty even to my ears. That was the beauty of insults and cuss words: they translated universally, no matter the meaning. She bucked and snarled like an animal, trying to push me off of her. I shifted my weight to press more firmly on her abdomen and chest.

Her eyes—metallic-gray with hints of green—bulged. "Get off," she spat in Universal, no doubt having caught on my race from the round pupils of my eyes. Her words were followed by a hard punch on my side. Since I was still pinning her right arm, that meant she punched my left soft side, and that was a hell of a punch. When she bucked again, I slid to the side and she took the opportunity to dislodge me. My grip on her wrist hadn't softened, however.

"Let go," she gritted, eyes moving behind me for a moment. "You want the blade?" Suddenly, she opened her hand and let the blade drop. "Keep it."

That threw me for the second it took my mind to realize that she was on a schedule and she needed to be moving. I let go of her arm and kicked her on the side of the head. She looked startled for a second before her eyes rolled back and she went limp.

"Ouch," Mac said. "That's going to hurt."

I bent down, checked her pulse—fast but steady—and pulled the scrunchie from my hair. In seconds, I had her wrists secured and her pockets emptied. There wasn't any identification on her person, but a peculiar device the size of my pinky with a series of small holes on one side and another Shivarhi blade.

Once done, I pulled the collar of my shirt and tucked my chin. There was a cut running from my right clavicle in a curve to the top of my armpit. It was bleeding freely, but it didn't look deep. A bit deeper and that blade would have cut through bone like it was butter.

"Now that I have your attention," Mac said, "you should know that the Kroz from the blue spire, Evo, is heading your way."

"The others?" I asked.

"Ravi responded to the text. He's in the university building along with Furox. Zafra is in the blue spire, and the rest are breaking up the crowd. He texted that you should stay out of it."

I pursed my lips. If I sent Ravi another text, he'd want to know where I was getting my information from. I could bluff my way with the previous tip, but not the second. I looked down at the unconscious Kroz.

I picked up the strange device and stuffed it in my pocket.

"How far is he?"

"He entered your building about thirty seconds ago. Given his pace and the distance you traveled, he should be upon you in thirty, twenty-nine, twenty-eight."

"You haven't cracked the firewall?" I asked as I ran up the stairs, aware that the Kroz approaching could probably hear my footsteps. I should have worn something with softer soles.

I reached the landing and turned onto the next level. I could hear now the footsteps behind me, quiet, almost silent. Had I been ordinary, I knew I wouldn't have heard them. I flattened myself against the wall and listened. Evo slowed when he neared my spot, no doubt trying to listen for my location.

I held my breath.

When he was almost upon me, I moved, leading with a high kick. I had to give it to him; the guy was fast. And seriously flexible. He bent backward, my foot missing his torso—dude was more than a head taller—by a hair's breadth. His hand snaked out for my leg and pulled, and I did a split, bounced, and flipped. This time, the heel of my foot connected with his chin. Unfortunately, it was the left leg.

Evo grunted and stepped back. He had on a balaclava that I didn't think he was wearing when he'd come into the building; otherwise, Mac would have said something.

I advanced on him, but suddenly I was flying in the air, shoved by a vicious force.

Telekinesis. Evo was a telekinetic—a damned powerful one. My head throbbed where it had struck the wall, and my back smarted like it was on fire.

Evo approached slowly. "Where is it?" he demanded in Universal.

I pushed sideways against the wall, gauging the distance between us and calculating my next move. Before I could stand, an invisible force grabbed me by the throat. "Where?" he growled.

The pressure around my neck constricted.

"Fight back!" Mac shouted. "Ignore the pain, ignore

everything! Get up."

Evo came another step closer. I struggled harder, and when he drew nearer still, I tackled his legs, managing to unbalance him. The pressure around my neck increased. For a terrifying moment, it felt like it would crush my larynx. Then it loosened. I gasped, unable to do anything more than pull desperate gulps of air.

Evo cursed and kicked me off him. I scrambled to my feet, ready to run—I had nothing effective against telekinesis. But there was no need.

Evo's head snapped up and he froze. Cursing, he pivoted on his heels and dashed away.

"That was anticlimactic," I rasped once he was out of sight.

"Are you okay?" Mac asked, his anxiety not quite masked.

"I will be," I reassured him just as two Kroz in full armor turned the corner, weapons raised.

"Don't fight them," Mac warned.

I raised my hands in the air. "Wasn't planning to," I said sub-vocally. "Can you track Evo?"

"I can't get access. I think someone messed up the system."

"Well, fuck. They must have rigged the security system so there wouldn't be any footage to incriminate them later. Track him from above when he exits the building."

"I'll try."

Chapter 13

I peered out the window of the hovercraft soaring above Cordolis, though the scenery no longer held any appeal. Mac had sent a photo of the unconscious Kroz woman to Ravi, and he'd summoned half his team to come for me.

Zafra had arrived moments after I'd surrendered to the first two Kroz, with Ravi not too long after that. I explained that I'd seen the woman pull the Shivarhi blade, texted him my suspicions about the trap, and followed her into the building. I told him about how she'd attacked me the moment we'd reached the stairwell. Ravi's eyes had flashed yellow at that, but he hadn't said anything.

Turned out Evo had sliced her throat before he'd come after me. I figured he was making sure the Kroz woman wouldn't be able to implicate him during questioning.

It also meant Evo hadn't been bluffing. He had meant to kill me.

I pointed in the direction Evo had gone, leaving out his identity and my strangulation. He never came out through any of the exits. Mac suspected Evo had left through an underground exit, but it wasn't like I could ask anyone about it. I let them give chase, knowing they wouldn't find anything.

Mac was scanning Cordolis through satellite view, but I wasn't so confident he'd find him, considering the size of the city and the number of people we'd seen earlier. The feeling of impotence left me in a foul mood.

Ravi checked that my injury was healing and headed in the opposite direction from his warriors and Evo. I'd have left out the injury from the Shivarhi blade, but the sliced jacket and the shirt underneath, both soaked with blood, gave it away.

It was only when we spotted the tall towers of the castle that I finally admitted I'd recognized the second Kroz who'd attacked me. I could see the denial in both Zafra and Furox's eyes, but instead of voicing a protest, Zafra pulled her commlink and brought up the profiles of her crew members.

"Third on the left," I told her.

Zafra's expression turned stony. "Evo," she spat and fisted her hand.

Furox slumped back into his seat. "I guess we'll be eating in the palace."

Zafra glanced up at me. "You okay with that?" she asked. "We can still do lunch after your injury is treated."

I wondered if the offer was just a formality or genuine. It sounded genuine, but I didn't know them enough to really tell. "Maybe another time," I replied. Not that my injury needed checking out—the intense itching and burning told me the skin was knitting fine. I wouldn't mind a change of clothes though. The slice hadn't been deep, but it had bled enough. "Maybe I can have lunch with Dolenta? The emperor approved a visit and I'd love to see her again." Besides, genuine or not, I had no doubt Zafra was itching to start the search for Evo. I would, if I were in her place. But Zafra only sent the details to Ravi and sat back.

Furox escorted me to my room while Zafra went to fetch Dolenta. Once again, I had expected to be taken to Dolenta's suite. But the princess was housed in the royal wing with the emperor, where only authorized Kroz, if any, were allowed.

After declining Furox's offer to clean my wound for the third time, he finally gave up, declared he'd return with lunch, and left. I wanted to tell him he didn't have to serve me, but I was hungry, and I'd already deprived him of his wife's company. I had ample time to wash and change clothes before Zafra arrived with the princess.

Dolenta came clad in the same dark armor as a royal warrior. It made sense that the emperor's daughter would have the best armor in existence. Besides the protection, the armor gave her enough anonymity to allow her some freedom. I only knew it was her by the power of deduction, considering Zafra had gone to fetch her. The only difference between the two was the height and the fact that where Zafra's entire armor was one piece—with the helmet smoothly retracting into the collar of the armor, seemingly at will—Dolenta's armor was two pieces.

Once the door of the room slid shut, Dolenta pulled off the helmet and tucked it under one arm. She smiled shyly at me and waved. "Hi," she said in that sweet, quiet voice.

"Hi back," I replied with a heartfelt smile, then turned to Zafra. "Do we wait for you, or will someone be coming for the princess?"

Zafra raised one eyebrow. "What do you mean, someone be coming for the princess?"

I blinked. "Don't you, you know…have work to do?"

Zafra's initial confusion cleared and she chuckled. "The princess is my duty. I'll be staying here."

"Oh, okay," I said, wondering if I was supposed to keep this visit short.

"You don't need to look so glum," Zafra said, moving toward the balcony. "I can sit out here if you'd like to spend time with the princess alone. The emperor gave clearance for that."

"No, that's not what I meant. I just thought you had better things to do than babysit us."

"The emperor trusts you with the princess alone," Zafra reiterated. "You went to great lengths to ensure that the princess returned home safely. But for now, we'll exercise caution until things settle down once more."

I inclined my head. "I understand. Please, come and have a seat with us." I motioned to the seating arrangement.

"I'll do that when the food arrives," she said and paused beside the divide between the bedroom and the balcony.

I turned back to the princess. "Come join me," I said, taking a seat.

"I wasn't sure if my father would pass on my request," Dolenta said timidly. "I'm glad he did. I wanted to see you again."

"He did," I confirmed, smiling. "But even if not, I'd have asked for permission to see you."

It wasn't entirely a lie. I'd have asked for permission, yes, but from Ravi, not the emperor. Given Dolenta's quiet pleasure, I knew it was the right thing to say. "How have you been?"

Like a switch turned off, her smile disappeared. Annoyance flashed in her expression, tinged with resignation. "I've been cooped up in my rooms with a sentry since I stepped foot on Krozalia. They follow me to the bathroom, refuse to let me sit outside on the balcony, and stand over my bed while I sleep." She flopped into the chair across from mine and sighed. "This is the first time I've walked out the royal residence and that's only because Chief Zafra gave the order."

I looked at Zafra, leaning against the opening to the balcony. To a casual onlooker, she'd look like someone bored out of her mind, but her location and the alertness in her eyes told another story. The emperor may have allowed Dolenta to have a private moment with me, but she wasn't going to be without a watch.

"It's all for your safety, Koshka," Zafra said soothingly.

"I know," Dolenta said and sighed. "I just…" She waved a hand. "Never mind. Lori said that tomorrow things would return to normal."

"Lori talks too much," Zafra admonished.

Dolenta raised her chin. "It's my life. I deserve to know what's going on."

The stare-down only broke when there was a knock at the door. Zafra straightened, wiggling fingers in a way I'd seen Kroz about to throw magic did. We waited until Dolenta had the helmet on before Zafra opened the door.

Furox stood there, blocking most of the entrance as he scanned the room. Assessment made, he winked at Dolenta and turned to the server behind him and the largest tray I'd ever seen, laden with covered domes.

"I'll take it from here," he stated. "Thank you."

The server bowed, backed away, then left.

"You ordered the entire pantry?" Zafra asked as Furox maneuvered the giant tray to the seating area.

"Just a bit of everything. I'm starving."

"You're always starving," Zafra joked and followed behind him.

Before anyone had a chance to fill a plate, Furox was eating, trying a piece of everything—roasted poultry, smoked fish, yellow rice, a medley of steamed vegetables, and a giant pie. I had a feeling the gluttonous behavior had a darker purpose: Furox was tasting for poison, the belief fortified by Zafra's lack of protest.

We ate mostly in silence, with a remark here and there about the food—the spices used, the comparison to the roast in the Flying Crown pub, and Dolenta's suggestion of which spice she preferred paired with which dish.

"If you want some of the pie," Zafra said as Dolenta sat back, "I suggest you take it with you. You should go back to your rooms."

"Do I have to?" Dolenta asked. She looked so desolate, my heart went out to her.

Zafra's expression softened. "You can visit another time. Right now, we have duties to attend and we're to escort you before we go."

"The execution?" I asked and regretted the question when something like grief flashed in Furox's eyes. If he was as close to Ravi as he seemed to be, then Thern's betrayal must have come as a blow. "I'm sorry," I said simply. There wasn't anything I could say or do to change what was going to happen.

They waited for Dolenta to put the helmet back on before strolling to the door.

"Thank you," I called after them. "For the company and the tour."

Furox waved his hand in the air, and Zafra gave me a distracted nod before her helmet covered her face.

Chapter 14

Lord Drax
"Sir, we lost him."

I looked up from the body I was examining to find Rodil and Firaz, the two warriors who had been closer to Leann's location when she had sent me an image of Flenna, the Kroz who had attacked her and a castle guard. She wasn't a royal warrior, but she was still based in the castle.

My attention snagged on the bloody Shivarhi blade beside the body. On the image Leann had sent, neither the blade nor the woman had any blood stains. Now, Flenna was sporting a bloody smile under her jaw.

Everything pointed back to the castle. Even the call-for-arms earlier had come from the castle, though I sure as hell hadn't sent out the command. Protests happened all the time, and the royal Kroz warriors rarely interfered. Someone in the castle had wanted us there. Leann was right—the warriors were the target.

Evo. How many more of my cadre were working for the rebellion? He was a good warrior, quiet and dedicated, his performance above average. I had sent Rodil and Firaz to his home to pick him up, but Evo had bolted the moment he'd spotted the two warriors. They'd let me know they were giving chase, but now here they were, reporting back with failure.

"Send out a summons for a meeting to the First Battalion, all divisions," I told them. "I want a meeting with everyone, virtually or in person, within the hour. I want you to document everyone's timelines, where they are, where they have been, who they were with, and report back as soon as it's done."

"Yes, sir." Rodil shifted, clearly uncomfortable.

"Yes?" I snapped. My patience with the entire situation and the lack of answers was running thin.

"Some of them might not like that," he said.

"Too bad. You note also whoever has a problem with the questions and send it to Lieutenant Furox or Chief Zafra—"

"He meant that others won't like that we're the ones conducting the interrogation, sir," Firaz interjected. "You know? We're still the youngest and newest members of your cadre."

I sat back on my haunches, the body of Flenna a mere meter away.

"You think that because you're the youngest, you lack the authority or respect you should have?" I demanded harshly.

Rodil swallowed. "No, sir."

"We'll go now," Firaz said, taking Rodil's wrist.

It was the fear in Rodil's eyes and the way Firaz acted—protective of the other warrior—that gave me pause. Twice during this brief exchange, Firaz had stepped in his defense, and I knew for a fact they were both fierce and skilled warriors.

Fear was a healthy reaction; it kept the warriors from jumping feet first into a dangerous situation without assessing it first. But this, this was fear of other fellow warriors, of following a command that could, in the worst case scenario, result in a clash. No warrior of my cadre had ever shown hesitation to brawl, regardless of injuries or broken limbs.

"Wait," I said, frowning. "Explain to me what you meant. Everyone in my cadre was handpicked and trained in the same manner. If you're a royal warrior, you've passed the same tests and examinations and training everyone else had. There's no one above another unless you're captain of a squad, and even so, you still answer to me. Explain why another warrior might not like that you're asking them what I ordered you to."

"I-I…it's nothing, sir," Rodil stammered.

I rose to my feet. "Rodil, you've been a member of my cadre for the past five years. Have I ever given you any reason to think that you can't speak your mind?"

"No, sir."

"Then what is it?" I demanded, watching the color drain from Rodil's face. "Speak," I snarled.

"Some of the warriors have been meeting in secret," Firaz said quickly and sidestepped Rodil's attempt to stop him. "When Rodil caught them earlier this year, they threatened his daughter's life if he reported anything."

I'd been watching Firaz as he spoke, but at the last part, my head whipped back to Rodil. "Who?"

"Please, sir. My daughter…"

"Will come to no harm. Do they have her?"

"No. She's with my mate, but someone is always there, watching the house. They…they leave presents for my daughter…on our front door, on her bed, even by the bathroom sink when she's showering. She thinks it's a game that her mother is playing but I know they're doing it to remind me they can get to her anytime, anywhere."

"How many were in this secret meeting?" I asked softly. "There's an execution taking place later today. Four are warriors: Conel, Sera, Yoney, and Riqla."

"They were there," Rodil whispered. "So were Vazra, Hamel, and Sol."

But not Evo. The rebellion probably rotated their meetings to accommodate schedules and to lessen suspicion. I pulled out my commlink and sent a text to Furox, Zafra, and my parents to head out and pick up those warriors for questioning. I hated to involve my parents, but I was at a loss about who was loyal and who wasn't.

"The people posted near your house?" I asked as I sent the text and an update to the emperor.

"There are three. I don't know who they are, but they switch every ten hours."

"Enforcers, mercenaries, thugs?"

"I don't know. They don't wear uniforms. They have no tribal tattoos or any type of identifiers."

I nodded and texted that as well. "What about you?" I

asked Firaz.

"I'm clear, sir."

"Good. Go and do what I said. Leave Vazra, Hamel, and Sol. They'll be dealt with. And Rodil? If this happens again and you don't report, your name will be added to the list for the following execution roster."

Imperial Stardust

Chapter 15

I had intended to go speak with Lorenzo after I'd returned from touring the Capital, but things hadn't gone as planned.

By the time I was alone in my room, I had no patience for his acerbic attitude. Still, I'd sent him a text explaining that the emperor had agreed to listen to the trade proposal and that he better be straightforward with the representative if he wanted to leave here with a signed agreement. The demands that I presented myself to the Blue Wing started almost immediately, but if I'd wanted to see Lorenzo, I wouldn't have sent him a text.

It was a while after Lorenzo stopped texting when I heard a rumbling sound, like something massive sliding on the ground. I looked up from the commlink I was playing with, but the seating arrangement hadn't moved. No, it was the wall beside the chest of drawers that had become a passageway.

Dolenta stood there, wearing a long coat with the hood up—and the mask she'd worn when she'd first boarded the *Splendor* all those weeks ago. I stood, stuffing the commlink in my pocket. "What is it?"

"Do you want to watch?"

I tilted my head, but before I could ask, she amended, "The execution. You asked about it. Do you want to watch it?"

"Weren't you complaining about your guards not leaving you alone?" I looked pointedly behind her at the dark and empty passageway.

Dolenta's mouth formed a sly half-smile. "You live with guards all your life, you learn how to evade them."

I smiled back. "I don't think that's a good idea. This isn't a game. I can sympathize with the way you're feeling constricted, but I can't fault the need for caution." I raised a hand and let it drop, unsure how to get through to her. "You know powerful people want you dead, and going out there without an escort is not a good idea."

Dolenta raised her chin. Inside the mask, her purple eyes gleamed. "I'm going. I want to see the faces of the people who killed my friends, who paid to have others kidnap me. I want to sleep at night knowing they're all gone." The latter was more a whisper, but I heard her loud and clear.

"Poor kid," Mac said. "I wonder if the emperor knows his daughter is having a hard time."

"I can call the guards—"

"They'll only take me back to my rooms."

"I can get in serious trouble if something happens to you. I wouldn't forgive myself if something did."

Dolenta lowered her head. "Very well." She turned to leave and I had a feeling it wasn't to go back to her room.

"I don't think she looked defeated enough," Mac observed. "Want to bet she plans to go alone?"

"We both know I'd lose that bet," I said sub-vocally.

I debated hunting down Furox or Zafra, but by the time I found either—if I found either—Dolenta would be long gone. And she didn't tell me where she planned to watch the execution. Why hadn't I asked for a direct way to contact the two warriors?

Cursing, I stomped into my boots and rushed into the passageway. The glint of triumph in Dolenta's purple eyes when I reached her told me I'd just been suckered. *But what else was I supposed to do?*

Mac chuckled. "That's positively diabolical. I need to take notes."

The secret door to the passageway slid shut the moment we turned the corner, plunging us into relative darkness. The only reason I could still see was because of my enhanced vision. I had a feeling Dolenta had no idea how limited we humans were.

"Where's the execution taking place?" I asked softly,

aware of the way sounds echoed in the narrow and lengthy passageway.

"In the East Arena. I know a place where we can watch and stay hidden."

"If your guards don't find us first," I muttered. And execute me as well.

"We have enough time," Dolenta assured me. "It'll take them a bit yet to find out I'm not in the shower, then some more before they can track me."

We traveled through the dark passages and up several stairwells for almost five minutes before I began hearing voices. They were faint but unmistakably belonged to a large crowd. It took another minute and the exit of the secret passageway into a circular room, open to the elements, for me to start making out the words. By the shape and the high elevation, I assumed we were in one of the high towers. Though, going by the dirt caked on the floor, no one had been here in a very long time.

"This was my mother's favorite spot," Dolenta told me, glancing around with a sad look in her eyes. "I haven't been here since…for a long time." She motioned to the flimsy edge that kept people from plunging to their death by a thin knee-high barrier. Dolenta crouched near the barrier and peered down.

I knelt beside her. There, far below but still several floors above ground level, was a stage facing several hundred people. On the stage was a familiar scene, though one I'd only watched on holograph vids and never with that amount of prisoners.

A Kroz, dressed in long dark robes with the hood obscuring his features, faced them. Behind the stage, stretching several meters to the side and up, a huge holograph played the scene for everyone else to watch. I also knew for a fact this would be broadcast to the rest of the galaxy. The Kroz wanted people to see and fear them, and this was their most powerful and effective tactic.

"Evo's not there," Mac observed.

No, he wasn't. Over to the side, a tall Kroz was listing the crimes of the prisoners. I counted, surprised to find fourteen of them.

"...they have been tried and found guilty of high treason against the monarchy for crimes of disloyalty, murder, conspiracy, levying of war against the government, the giving of aid and comfort to the enemies. By Section 63 of the Crime and Disorder Act, the punishment for such crimes is sundering of the body and soul."

The Kroz motioned with a hand, bowed, then moved back. The executioner stepped forward. Even dressed in the black robe with the hood drawn, I didn't need Mac's whispered words in my ears to recognize Ravi—or rather, the Grim Reaper of the Galaxy.

He paused in front of one of the prisoners. To the onlooker, he seemed to be looking down at him. On the holographic vid, I recognized Thern's bowed head and felt a pinch of sympathy for Ravi and the grief he no doubt was feeling.

"He looks bigger with the robes," I murmured, trying to identify something from the Kroz I knew.

Dolenta cast me a sideways look. "He told you? I didn't think he was allowed to reveal his identity to anyone."

I cleared my throat and inwardly winced, forgetting that the only reason I knew the Grim Reaper's identity was because Mac had done some hacking the moment we'd entered the Krozalian system.

"I guess it makes sense," Dolenta continued thoughtfully, "considering the life-mate bond."

That was the second time someone had alluded to that, and coming from the mouth of a teenager, I had a sinking feeling it wasn't the misconception I'd first assumed.

"What exactly does this life-mate thing mean?"

Dolenta shrugged. "It's a life bond between mates." She nodded at the arena below. "It's starting."

I wanted to push for more, but when I looked down, I was transfixed. I'd watched this play a few dozen times from holographic vids—there was at least one execution a year—but watching the play with my own two eyes and knowing the people on that stage personally changed my perspective.

Ravi had his arms to the sides as if he was hugging an invisible tree trunk, his head lowered. In the holograph, the cowl obscured his features, making him look more sinister and mysterious. The traitors were all kneeling, heads also bowed. No one seemed to be putting any pressure on them, but there had to be some. I couldn't imagine myself kneeling and waiting for someone to execute me.

The air on the stage seemed to be distorting, like heat off hot metal, but that was clearer in the holograph. In fact, from up here, things seemed mild in comparison.

The execution, when it happened, was abrupt, lacking blood or any gore.

One moment Ravi was half bent, the next, he raised his head and threw his arms open to both sides. The fourteen kneeling Kroz convulsed, then broke into atoms and particles. For a few seconds, the air distortion looked thicker, but then slowly, it began to dissipate. Within two minutes, there was nothing left of the traitors but memories.

I shivered and stared at the empty stage where the prisoners had been. There once, then gone. Just like that, with one gesture—by one person.

Ravi lowered his arms and, as if a spell broke, the spectators applauded and shouted their approval, the sound thunderous, even from up in the tower. We watched until the spectators began dispersing, quickly and orderly. It reminded me of the riot in the city, and how Mac and I had debated about it. Maybe the Kroz did practice for these things.

I glanced back at the stage and found Ravi still standing, hands loose to his sides, head bowed. Mourning the loss of people he'd considered family once.

"Time to go, princess." I forced myself to look away from Ravi's lonely figure. I should have felt revulsion for what he did, fear for what he could do—the power that he could one day be ordered to use on me—but I couldn't help but feel sorry for him. He looked dejected, like a man who'd lost everything. That image stayed with me all the way through the narrow passageways.

Back in my room, I found myself restless, so I left to see Cassandra and Sullivan. Lorenzo opened the door this time, and I told myself I could suffer his presence if it meant I wasn't left alone.

"The Minister of Trade came by today," Lorenzo began, and I paused in the act of passing him by. "He said that you spoke with the emperor about the Kukona mineral on the Confederacy's behalf."

"I hope you did what I said and were straightforward." When Lorenzo didn't reply, irritation sparked inside my chest. "Fine. Don't blame me if they refuse then."

I was halfway through the living room when he spoke. "I want you to attend the negotiations from now on."

I frowned at him over my shoulder. "I don't think that's a good idea."

"The emperor is obviously impressed with you, or impressed enough that he's willing to listen to you. You will attend the negotiations and speak on the Confederacy's behalf."

Cassandra appeared from the third door to the left as I turned to fully face him. "Lorenzo, I—"

"*Commodore* Lorenzo. And that's an order, soldier."

"Lorenzo," I repeated with patience I didn't know I had. "I don't think you understand that you have no authority over me. You didn't ten years ago and you still don't. I'm not"—I raised my voice when he opened his mouth to speak—"going to attend the negotiations because I'll do or say something that will break whatever trade you're trying to broker. I'm not good with politicking; I'm not good with kissing ass. I spoke with the emperor because I found an opportunity to do so and because I trust that the CTF is trying to prevent war and the unnecessary loss of life. I'm not your lackey, and I'm not a subordinate, so stop trying to push me around."

"Or what?"

"That's enough," Sullivan snapped from behind me, preventing me from saying things I knew would come back to screw me over.

Lorenzo's death glare moved past me to where I assumed Sullivan was standing.

"You're going about this the wrong way, Commodore," Sullivan spat.

"I outrank you," Lorenzo spat in return. "All of you. And I'll be putting everything that's happened during this mission into my report."

"Yes, yes. You do that. But with all due respect, here in Krozalia, Clara—Leann—has more power than you do. You want her help, at least have the decency to be civil."

Lorenzo's face reddened.

I shifted, ready to tackle him if he tried to attack, but he didn't.

Instead, he surprised me. "Captain Colderaro," he ground out, "I'd appreciate it if you could accommodate us and attend the next stage of our negotiations. Would you be so gracious as to oblige us?"

I swallowed a chuckle. But Lorenzo was trying, and I didn't want him to look at Sullivan with an I-told-you-so look that proved I couldn't be reasoned with.

"Fine. But keep in mind if I say something that sets back the negotiation, that I did give you fair warning."

"Just be there," Lorenzo said tightly. "Your presence means you support the trade and for some reason I can't fathom, that means something to the Kroz."

All my humor fled with those words. The KKM wasn't something the Kroz traded lightly, and they would be more vigilant now than ever. "Make sure to explain to the Kroz exactly what the CTF wants with it. I mean it, Lorenzo. The KKM is not something the Kroz trade lightly. You want it, you give them a reason to agree. Otherwise, I promise you that they'll send you packing empty-handed and refuse any further talks."

Lorenzo's eyes narrowed. "Why? What do you know?"

"Only that the Kroz would obliterate the CTF if you mishandle the KKM."

He waited for me to elaborate, his gaze searching my face, but when I said nothing more, he retreated to his room, shutting the door behind him.

"Well, that didn't go so badly," Sullivan said.

"I didn't mean to put you in the spot like that," I said in return. We moved to the blue sofa that I suspected the wing was named after.

"He'll get over it."

"He'll make you pay for it," I warned.

Sullivan sighed. "He'll try. The worst he can do is slap me on the wrist." When his words didn't ease my concern, Sullivan gave me a small smile that crinkled the corners of his eyes. "It's not my first rodeo with him. We've been at odds for over a decade."

Since they'd left Alex and me in the asteroid.

"Now, I heard you had a chat with the emperor himself. Why don't you tell us all about it? Cassie's been nagging and nagging for us to go track you down."

"We did," Cassandra muttered. "But we got lost." She slumped beside me and closed her eyes. "We had to be rescued by a servant who either pretended not to understand us or has been ordered not to let us wander the castle."

For some reason, I imagined Vera escorting them back and acting like she didn't speak Universal. "If it's any comfort, it took me a long time to find you guys too. I got lost a few times, even after I was given directions to the Blue Wing by several Kroz."

"What's with the name anyway?" Sullivan asked and we all snickered.

Cassandra groaned. "To have reached Krozalia and have nothing to say about it. I just wish, since we've come all this way, that we could do some sightseeing. It doesn't need to be in the palace if that's off-limits. How do the ordinary Kroz live? What do they do in their day-to-day? How do they pass their time? What are their shops like?"

Sullivan snorted and flopped on the seat beside hers. "You're just itching to explore the shops and the food."

Cassandra's expression took on a dreamy look. "I mean, have you tasted their food? I can't believe how many different flavors I was missing until I tried them out."

I sat back and smiled as she rambled about all the different dishes they had tasted since arriving.

"I'll see if I can wrangle up a trip to the city for you guys," I offered.

Cassandra sprang from her seat with a squeal and threw herself at me.

I patted her on the back gently. "I didn't say I was going to take you. I'd get lost within the hour. It's a megalopolis out there, sprawling horizontally and vertically, and even underwater."

"You went out?" Sullivan asked, leaning forward and propping his elbows on his knees. "Tell us. I bet holographic images don't compare."

"I had a brief tour above the city earlier, but honestly, there's so much out there, it's easier to describe it as a whole than in detail."

"Tell us what you saw then," Cassandra urged, resuming her seat beside me. "Our view from here is either of the ocean or the tall trees. It's beautiful and reminds me of home, but I want to experience the advanced technology the Kroz are renowned for."

So I did, as best as I could. The never-ending bridge to Sarkar, the spiral towers reaching for the stars, the multitude of colors and people, even the tracks that had clamped around the university building to facilitate our descent. I hadn't expected to have enough to say, but Cassandra and Sullivan had enough questions to keep us talking for hours. Even Lorenzo had come out to listen and ask questions, and for once, he kept his attitude civil.

By the time I left, it was dark outside, though I couldn't

tell the time, or even what constituted "late" in Krozalia.

Chapter 16

I found Ravi in my room when I returned. He was just sitting there in the chair where I usually sat to eat, so it was a bit of a jolt.

I recovered quickly enough, letting the door slide silently shut behind me as I took him in, legs stretched and crossed at the ankles, hands resting atop each other on his belly.

He looked relaxed and at ease. I wasn't fooled. It was the drooping of his shoulders and shadows under his heavy-lidded eyes that told me how exhausted he really was. That, and the way his eyes looked more yellow than umber. I'd figured out in the past few weeks that the yellow came out whenever his emotions were running high. Like passion, anger, sadness.

"Enjoyed your time?" he asked, and for a moment I thought he was talking about the sundering back in the East Arena. "I was half expecting you to stay with them tonight."

"If I did?"

"Then I'd have felt like a fool for staying and waiting for you."

Warmth at his words spread in my chest. I forced myself to move and take the seat across from his. "You look tired," I observed aloud.

"I *am* tired. It was a long day."

A fist of emotions tightened around my stomach. Pleasure and excitement at the knowledge that he chose to unwind with me after a hard day.

"I watched the execution…with Dolenta," I added the latter because I thought he should know the kid had her means to slip around the castle.

Ravi sighed. "I know." His gaze locked with mine, a deep assessment that made me uncomfortable, but not enough for me to look away. "You know what I am."

"I do," I admitted.

"Does it bother you?" The question sounded curious, but the caution in his eyes told me my answer was important.

"It does," I began, pausing when his expression shuttered. "Ravi—"

"It's fine," he interjected. "My ability isn't something people feel comfortable about. My mother ran away from my father when she discovered what he was."

My eyebrows knitted together. "Your father?"

"It's a family thing. My father took over as executioner from his mother, his mother from her uncle, and so on. When my father retired, I inherited the mantle."

"Oh, I thought it's always been you."

Ravi's mouth quirked. "We've had an executioner for the past eight hundred years. I'm not that old. My parents aren't that old. Hell, the emperor isn't that old."

"How old are you?"

"It depends. Our lifespans are longer than yours. Our years also differ from yours in various aspects; our days, years, and seasons are longer than human years. I'm a hundred-and-two, but in human terms, that's equivalent to thirty-something."

"I'm—never mind." I studied his features, but he didn't look like someone who had already lived more than a hundred years. "You inherited the executioner mantle. Did you want to?"

Ravi exhaled and looked away. "It's not a matter of want, but rather of who develops the sundering affinity."

"And you did," I murmured.

"In a manner of speaking."

"But did you want it?"

His wariness returned. "It doesn't matter if I wanted it or not. It's who I am."

"No, it isn't." Before he could withdraw even more, I stood, straddled his lap, and placed both palms over his stubbled cheeks. "Look at me." I waited until he did, wanting him to see the sincerity in my eyes as well as hear it in my voice. "This bothers me, but only because this responsibility is on your shoulders when it clearly takes a toll on you. No one should carry such a burden, especially against people you cared about."

Ravi's eyes closed as he exhaled, and his hands gripped my waist.

"I'll never harm you," he vowed softly. "I'll never let anyone harm you."

I lowered my head and touched my mouth to his. Just a soft brush of lips as I looked into his eyes from inches away. This close, I could see different colors in his irises, flecks of gold and brown and orange, more subtle in the glow of the yellow.

"I believe you," I murmured.

His hands tightened and exhaustion switched to hunger a second before his mouth captured mine. His tongue traced my lip, demanding entry, and I let him in, swiping my tongue over his. The sound that escaped him provoked all sorts of reactions inside me—emotionally and physically. The vibration of his deep groan against my chest, his wandering hands. Lights exploded, stars realigned, and something inside me expanded at the same time everything inside me clenched. The experience was one I'd never felt before, deliciously exquisite.

He broke the kiss first, sliding his mouth against my cheek. He breathed against my ear, his hands moving up and down over my sides. "You test my control, Leann," he whispered. "It's best if I go now."

I shivered and slid my hand over his chest and around his neck. "Stay tonight."

Ravi swallowed loudly. "It's not proper," he began.

I groaned. "Fuck proper," I said and pulled his mouth back to mine. But he refused to let me deepen the kiss and take it to the passionate level from a few moments ago. Instead, he kept it gentle and tender, and it was just as devastating.

"I have to go," Ravi repeated, nipping my bottom lip. "You're more tempting than I have the strength to resist tonight."

"Then don't resist," I breathed against his lips.

He groaned. "That's not how things are done here," he said, pushing me back to look me in the eyes.

That gave me pause. I scanned his face to figure out if he was saying what I thought he was saying. "Are you telling me that you never…you know…before?"

Humor entered his eyes and tilted the corners of his mouth. "I've been attracted to other women before. I've had flings. I've had one-night stands. I've had long relationships."

I scowled at him. "How is this thing between us different?"

The mirth in his eyes dwindled like a smothered ember. He grabbed my hand and pressed it against his steadily beating chest. "How much do you know about Kroz anatomy?"

"I know you have an extra vocal cord that helps you speak magic?" It came out as a question. Although I'd seen him work magic before, I'd never heard him chanting or speaking as he did.

"You can say that. We call it our Ashak. When we do magic, we exhale magic out and shape it with our hands, direct it with our eyes, or even will, for the more powerful ones. But we also have the Carindum, which is essentially a smaller heart that is born inactive, and stays frozen until the day we form a life-mate bond."

I tilted my head and he tucked the hair that fell behind my ear. "When a Kroz meets a mate-match, that heart becomes active." He flattened my hand over his heart and pressed. I felt it then. Underneath the steady thump of his heart, something else was beating.

Thump-bum. Thump-bum. Thump-bum.

"It began beating after our first kiss back on your ship."

Memories of the moment in question flashed in my mind. The way he'd broken the kiss, the look of shock in his eyes as he'd rubbed his chest—just exactly where my palm lay. Thump-bum. Thump-bum. Thump-bum.

I had no idea what to say, where to begin, if he expected

me to be thrilled or not. So, I voiced the least damaging question in my mind. "It's a bit slow, isn't it?"

"It's usually slower…a beat or two every other minute, but with the two of us this close, it…" he exhaled and finished. "The closer we are, the more intimate we get, the faster the Carindum will beat."

"If we sleep together, this bond will set in?"

"No. There's a ritual before that," he said. A wicked glint danced in his eyes as he pulled my hand to his mouth and kissed the center of my palm. I felt the touch like a tug to the soles of my feet. My hands had never been an erogenous zone.

"If a Kroz finds his mate-match," he explained, "it's customary to wait until after the ritual to consummate the bond. It's a respect thing, a sign of commitment."

"What happens after the ritual?"

"Our lives would be intertwined with each other's."

"But I'm not a Kroz. I have only one heart."

Ravi shrugged a shoulder. "It doesn't matter. Once the bond sets, my life will be irrevocably tied to yours. The only way for it to break is if one of us dies first."

"That's what happened to the emperor. Can't he form a new bond?"

"No. Once the Carindum stops beating, it begins to shrivel. Most die within a week, but some, like the emperor, can draw strength from the planet's core and slow the necrosis of the tissue."

"Why would anyone make themselves so vulnerable?" I wondered.

Ravi's expression closed off, and I wanted to take back my words.

Instead, I plunged on. "Why form that bond when you can…marry someone and have all the benefits and none of the drawbacks?"

"A life-mate bond isn't a liability. Bonded pairs draw strength from each other as well. It's a connection not many can form, but very few walk away from. My parents have been mated for over three centuries now."

"Hm-mmm," I murmured.

I recalled Mac telling me the lifespan of an average Kroz was around seven centuries, double that for a mated pair. I still wasn't convinced the longevity was worth it. Maybe he was right and not rushing this bond thing was for the best. Sooner or later, I'd leave Krozalia, and where would that put us? I aged slowly, I knew that, but I was still aging. What did that mean for him? Or would it affect both of us equally, regardless of the race difference? Would we need to be within a certain distance of each other to survive or endure being apart?

My thoughts and doubts must have shown on my face because Ravi stood, pulling me off his lap, and settling me down gently on my feet. "I should go."

"Ravi—"

"I can't do this, not to me and not to you without a commitment."

"When I leave," I began.

He placed his palm over my mouth, eyes searching. "Don't. Don't say anything. Just give me a chance. If at the end you still think you're not ready, then—then go. But give me the chance to change your mind first."

I nodded after a second, and he lowered his hand, brushed his lips over mine, and turned to go, stopping at the door. "There's a memorial ritual tomorrow for the crew I lost. It would be an honor to me if you attended with me."

"I'll be there," I promised, then watched him slide out the door and disappear.

"You have feelings for him," Mac said after some time.

I grunted. "I shouldn't. Nothing will come of this but heartache."

"You could stay, if you want it enough."

I scowled at the empty room. "You, of all people, know that's a horrible idea."

"Why?"

"We have a task."

"That you set for yourself. One day, you'll have to let Alex and this revenge go. Why can't that day be today?"

***

When Zafra came knocking in the morning, I'd thought she was there to escort me to the memorial ritual. She had her armor on again, and I wondered if she ever took it off. I'd yet to see Ravi in his, so maybe wearing it was a matter of personal preference.

"I'm your escort for today," she announced when the door opened.

"Am I dressed right?" I asked awkwardly, unsure if there was a dress code for the memorial ritual.

Zafra looked at my black pants, black long-sleeve t-shirt, and black combat boots. "I don't know much about human traditions, but here in Krozalia, you can wear anything you'd like to breakfast," she paused, considering it, then added, "unless you're going to a fancy restaurant. Which we aren't. If you want fancy food, you'll have to ask Ravi to take you."

I leaned back against the bedpost. "Breakfast. I thought you were here to take me to the memorial ritual."

Zafra froze. "He invited you?"

I straightened. "Was he not supposed to?" I countered. "It's fine if not. I don't want to disrupt the ritual."

"No, no. It's fine. It's just that..." Zafra exhaled a long breath and gave me a lingering look. "I guess he's more serious about you than I wanted to believe. My fault, because he did say...well, never mind." She entered the room fully and let the door slide shut behind her.

I tried to parse her words in my head but could only come up with one conclusion. "You don't approve." Oddly, the realization made me somewhat disappointed. I'd never been a people-pleaser, never tried to find myself in the spotlight or be anyone's bestie. On the contrary, I was a lone person whose friendships resulted from happenstance.

"It's not my place to approve or disapprove. But," she scanned my face for something. "He's not as cold-hearted as he likes people to think he is. If this isn't something you're serious about, let him know." She crossed the room to the sitting arrangement and took a seat. "Now, let me see what else you have to wear for the memorial ritual."

I glanced down at my clothes as if, for some reason, they'd have morphed into something else. "I'm guessing this isn't appropriate?"

"You're guessing right."

"Then I don't have anything. I only packed three changes of clothes."

"We can go to your ship—"

I was shaking my head before she could finish. "I don't have anything dissimilar to this. I spend my days alone in my ship, taxiing people and resources from station to station. My wardrobe consists of traveling clothes and jumpsuits."

Zafra pulled herself upright. "Then we'll get you something." She looked me up and down, an assessing look that would have been condescending on anyone else. "You're too short for my clothes to fit, but I know a place that will get you ready within a zap." She snapped her thumb and forefinger together and motioned at the door. "Shall we?"

"Now?"

"Well, we can have breakfast first," she said thoughtfully, placing a hand over her belly. "I'm starving."

I hesitated a moment. "I don't know what Ravi told you, but you don't need to babysit me. I can take care of myself."

Zafra smiled. It made her look so much younger and approachable. "He said something like that." She waved a hand, grabbed my arm, and pulled me behind her. "But I'm going for breakfast. Furox is probably already ordering, and I do want to get to know the woman who's managed to get my brother twisted into knots."

I thought she was exaggerating. Ravi seemed level-headed to me, but I didn't know Ravi from before he'd approached me at V-5 Station. It wasn't even like we'd spent that much time together. He'd been mostly distant during the journey here, and last night had been our first time alone since we'd arrived. But there had been some moments…

…I sighed inwardly. It was true. Back on the *Splendor*, Ravi hadn't been this protective of me. He hadn't even shown his interest until I'd made a comment about it weeks into the voyage.

We were almost to the castle's entrance when I came to an abrupt halt. "We're going out?"

Zafra gave me a puzzling glance. "Yes. You don't want to?"

"No, I mean, yes. But is it possible to bring Cassandra and Sullivan along?"

"The Confederacy crew that came with you? Sure, but let's hurry before Furox decides we're not coming and eats all the food."

We didn't go to Cordolis. Instead, we took a small road down to the south of the castle, where a charming small town was nestled. Zafra was in a hurry to reach the Flying Crown, the tavern where Furox was waiting. Our tour yesterday was supposed to conclude there, a fifteen-minute walk downhill from the castle.

Rather than hiking down the scenic view—which was what most townsfolk did—we took a hovercraft. Zafra promised we could trek the return trip after we shopped for formal wear for the memorial ritual.

The tavern was open and airy and smelled wonderful. Furox had commandeered one of the tables in the back, where more prestigious patrons reserved seats or the entire room, depending on the party. Although it was much smaller than the front room, it accommodated two dozen tables, done in dark wood with intricate carvings. The flooring was made of polished wood, the same as the walls, also with decorative engravings. It had floor-to-ceiling windows on two sides, overlooking the cliffs and the sea, making the room brighter and cheerier despite the darker tone of the wood.

Furox stood closer to the windows, pushing two tables together while a server placed dishes on the table. He looked up when we entered, eyes passing over the group before lighting up with a smile. "I'm glad you all could make it."

"No you're not," Zafra quipped. "You were hoping we'd be late so you could eat half the food."

"Nonsense. I'd have simply savored a few bites with my mate."

Zafra glanced around. "Where is she?"

"Putting Derk to sleep. He was cranky because he couldn't sleep last night."

Zafra took a middle seat. "Why not?"

"Seems like he's teething. I didn't know babies could scream that loud." He dropped onto the seat beside hers with a sigh. "It was a scary thing to witness."

"What?" Zafra teased. "You can't handle a crying baby?"

Furox glanced at her, his expression serious. "I would kill anyone who dared make my son cry like that. But last night, I was helpless, unable to do anything but watch as he suffered. It's awful, not being able to soothe."

Cassandra took the seat next to him. "Mom would give my brothers cold peaches to calm the gums and help with the ache. They always quieted after that."

Furox cocked his head. "We have some remedies my mate used, but they're all non-edible. I'll tell her to try it." He pulled out his commlink and stood. "Thank you."

"Fatherhood changed him," Zafra mused thoughtfully as we watched him go.

"It does most people," Cassandra agreed as she studied the spread and rubbed her hands together. "Now, tell me what these culinary delights are as I try them."

Furox returned some minutes later and resumed his seat, looking less stressed than when we'd arrived.

Conversation revolved around what the Kroz food was and how it was prepared, and while everyone tried bites of everything, Lorenzo and I ate only the things we recognized. The gesture didn't go unnoticed, but no one cracked a joke or made a comment about it.

"We'll go to the shop here in town first," Zafra told me

once most of the food was gone. "If Esme can't accommodate us, I'll take you to a shop in Cordolis."

"You're going shopping?" Cassandra squealed. "I'd like to come too, can I?" She aimed the latter at Zafra.

"I'm only buying one outfit," I said even as Zafra agreed, and the two began planning what I'd need, which colors looked better on me, the makeup I should or shouldn't use.

Sullivan punched me on the arm and made me spill some of the tea I was holding. "Imagine that, Captain Clara Colderaro is going to do something girly."

Lorenzo snorted. "Under duress," he added under his breath.

Even Furox chuckled.

I ignored the banter, hunched over my drink, and started to regret my promise to Ravi.

Chapter 17

"This town began as a collection of shacks built for the families of some of the employees of the castle," Zafra said as we crossed a narrow street. "They preferred not to live in the hustle and bustle of the castle life. It was private enough, cozy enough, that a trend started—guards, kitchen staff, and even some of the advisors—relocated their families here. Soon, shops began opening, a bar here, a bakery there, a hotel for visiting families."

Zafra pointed to a few crooked buildings, their pointy spirals seeming like they'd topple with the next strong gust of wind. "That's the oldest part of town, built some six centuries ago. It's also where some of the oldest tribe heads still reside." She motioned to a squat building that seemed out of place among all the spiral-shaped structures. "That's Esme's shop. She comes from a talented line of seamstresses and is a good friend of the family."

The building looked shabby from the outside, the windowpanes opaque, though I couldn't be sure if it was by design or age. A bell rang somewhere in the back when Zafra opened the door, and the smell of dry fabric and wood polish wafted out. The interior was well-lit and clean, but seriously cluttered. Silicon mannequins were everywhere, in every shape—bipedal, quadruped, hunched, thin, tentacled. Stands were placed between them, alongside racks stocked with garments protected by a white film.

A hunched, horned woman came out of the backroom, thin lips stretching to both sides when her red glowing eyes rested on Zafra.

"Zafra, my beautiful Koshka," she called in accented

Universal.

"You flatter me, Esme," Zafra responded.

"She's a Feromantic," Mac said, anticipating my confusion.

I'd never encountered the species before. Never really seen images anywhere in the database the CTF kept for known alien races.

Her biometrics scrolled on my right vision as Mac summarized the characteristics of the race.

"She's one of only a handful of survivors from Sector 2. They're amiable but can be vicious when threatened." The scrolling of information continued as Zafra greeted the seamstress with genuine warmth.

Omnivores—rodents are a delicacy.

Yuck.

Feromantics have a mild disposition that can turn violent when provoked.

"Some of the old ones have poisonous claws they introduce to their victims through scratches," Mac explained. "The deeper the scratch, the stronger the dose. It can paralyze their prey in seconds. Depending on the dosage, their victims will stay paralyzed for up to a whole week."

"Your presence in my shop is always a bright moment in my gloomy, unending day," Esme was saying.

"They're Parthenogenetic, but they rarely choose to reproduce," Mac went on. "They're highly intelligent and have an agility most overlook on account of the fact that they're very lazy."

Cassandra and I kept a step behind Zafra. I paid attention to her social cues so I wouldn't offend Esme by accident and listened to Mac's list of the Feromantics attributes.

Esme extended a spindly arm to Zafra. It was covered in green hair, tipped in what seemed like retractable claws. "To what do I owe your delightful presence? Your mother told me you ran off on a lethal last-minute call not so long ago. I trust the disturbance has been terminated, never to darken your mind again?"

Zafra brought the hand to her shoulder. The claws remained tucked in, but they were seriously close to her vulnerable jugular. "It was. Thank you for your concern."

"That's a sign of respect for the Feromantic elders," Mac remarked. "Putting one to their mercy and showing their trust."

Esme dropped her arm and stepped back with a low bow. "Your faith humbles these old bones, my lady."

"No need for formalities, Esme. You're family."

Esme loosened the bow, but her shoulders remained tucked in. Not once during the exchange did her eyes stray behind Zafra to where Cassandra and I stood.

"What can I do for you?"

"I'm here for memorial ritual attire," Zafra explained. "But I'm afraid there's no time for anything custom-made."

Esme straightened to her full height and sniffed. Like that, she was as tall as Zafra, which put her about a head taller than me.

"Why? What did you do with the last one I made you? You went gallivanting in the woods with that savage cousin of yours, didn't you? It had dragoski silk in it. You weren't supposed to go hunting with it. Honestly, you should have more sense than that vicious relative. You'd think a mate and a child would have tamed him, but apparently not."

I had a feeling she was talking about Furox and hid a smile at her description. I wouldn't go as far as to say he was savage, but he gave out a definite wild vibe.

Zafra was shaking her head and trying to get a word in, but the woman continued with her tirade. "It was one of my best designs. Your Mada bid me spare no cost and now here you are, wanting a new one."

Zafra finally put her hand on my back and pushed me forward. "It's for her; she's attending the ritual with Madrovi."

That quickly shut the woman up. She turned her glowing red eyes to me and appraised me from head to toe. Goosebumps broke over my body and I was glad for the long sleeves. I didn't want to insult the woman who'd be dressing me for an event I was beginning to suspect was much more than just a simple funeral march.

"When's the ritual?" Esme asked me.

"Um." I glanced at Zafra for the answer.

"In about three hours."

Esme squawked. Her head swiveled to Zafra and the red eyes narrowed. "And you're only bringing her to me now? Did you try all the shops on Atek Avenue first and when they turned you down, you decided I was your last choice?"

"No, of course not. I just didn't know my brother had extended the invitation until a few moments ago."

The glare swiveled my way and I suppressed the urge to raise my palms and move back. Not all the races took the gesture as one of surrender, and I didn't know enough about the Feromantics to determine which one the motion fell under. "It was a last-minute invitation," I said weakly, ignoring Cassandra's snicker behind me. "If it can't be done, it's fine. I'll tell Ravi I won't be able to make it—"

A spindly arm looped around mine and pulled me forward. "You'll tell Lord Drax no such thing." She continued pulling me further into the back of the shop. "I'll not have him begin courtship with a bedraggled human who looks like a beaten soldier just returned from war."

"Hey, my clothes are clean and fit me well."

Esme scoffed. "You look like a beggar playing dress-up."

I glanced back at Zafra and Cassandra, the former trying to stifle a grin and failing and the latter not even bothering to hide her wide smile. Before we turned the corner, Cassandra gave me two thumbs up and Zafra's guffaws finally broke loose.

Chapter 18

Lord Drax

"It's not a good idea," I said, fully aware that the emperor had set his mind. "You can't abdicate. Dolenta is still a child."

"I'll be her regent," the emperor said, not for the first time. "This will allow the transition of power to happen while I guide my daughter. As the empress, she'll have the power of the Tanue behind her, and the rebellion will have no choice but to relent."

"Your Carindum might not endure the stress," I tried next, feeling like an ass for pointing it out. But it was true. The only reason the emperor was able to hold on after his mate's death was because the Tanue gave him the strength he needed. If he severed that connection, his health would deteriorate much faster.

"I can hold on for a few years more," the emperor assured me. "Even after I abdicate, the effects of the connection with the Tanue will linger. It will give me enough time to guide her for a decade, at least. But in the event something happens, Ozvie has agreed to step in my stead."

I clenched my teeth and glared at my father. He shouldn't be encouraging what was essentially a slow suicide mission. The moment Dolenta assumed the throne and his connection to the Tanue broke, his Carindum would stop and begin atrophying, lingering effects or not.

"The power shift will give my daughter the time she'll need. It'll also give her the boost she currently lacks to start manipulating her Ashak with more accuracy. With the Tanue's initial protection, she'll be impervious to any attack. That's if the rebellion doesn't desist once she's crowned."

"I think it'll work," my father chimed in. He was no longer the Head Advisor, but his input was always welcome. "As it is now, the power of the throne is unbalanced. It makes the emperor and his heir a target. If he abdicates and the princess assumes the throne, the Tanue will keep her safe. It'll buy her the time she needs to mature into her power."

"Linsky and Zefron haven't made any suspicious moves," the emperor added. "I assume they are planning to lie low and wait for us to believe the rebellion is over before they try something new. This is our best chance."

I rubbed the palms of my hands over my face. "This could backfire. The rebellion might be pressured into making a move. We don't have enough information to counter their attack. It could be dangerous."

The emperor stood. "That's why we'll do this at once. We'll make the announcement late tonight, and the coronation early in the morning."

"I think we're all overlooking a crucial step here," my mother interjected, and at the emperor's nod, continued. "You're all assuming that the princess has the fortitude to see this through. What if she isn't ready—at least mentally—to take up the Tanue? You know the mind, if not the body, has to be strong enough for the task."

"You're right as always," the emperor agreed, clasping his hands behind his back. "Dolenta has known this day would come since the day we buried her mother. I've made sure she understands what will be asked of her. My daughter is ready. She has been ready for three years."

Chapter 19

When Ravi arrived to pick me up a few hours later, I was completely unprepared. For some reason, I had been expecting Zafra to escort me to the memorial ritual. But I shouldn't have. What really took me off guard, however, was Ravi's attire.

When Zafra had told me pants and long sleeves weren't appropriate for the memorial ritual, I'd assumed everyone would be dressed up. Except, Ravi wasn't. Oh, his pants and shoes were dressy enough, but from the waist up, he was naked. His chest and arms were slick, gleaming with oil, his hair styled away from his face. I'd seen him shirtless before, during workouts in the long journey to Krozalia; I'd even sparred with him once. But this, this felt different, more intimate, the two of us, standing there by the bedroom door. The smell of cinnamon and smoke and clean male invaded my senses, making my throat dry. I licked my lips and his eyes zeroed in on my mouth at once.

"You came. Zafra took me shopping. I hope this is okay?" I smoothed a clammy hand on the dress.

His warm, umber eyes roved over me. The slow perusal felt like a velvet caress, first down, then up. His eyes changed colors as they moved. By the time he met my eyes again, his were heavy-lidded and bright yellow with appreciation.

It made me feel exposed, in a sexy kind of way. The dress Esme had found for me wasn't something alien or too revealing, just a simple sheathe with a high collar and embroidered sleeves. Esme had claimed it had been made for a client who didn't like the simple, straight-cut lines and nipped waistline. I didn't mind the simplicity—on the contrary, I preferred it. The only thing that made the black dress stand out was the embroidered art: a sinewy creature that looked like a combination of a scaly green and red crocodile and a dragon. It had yellowish spikes in its back, colored wings, pointy white horns, and cat bristles. It contorted around the dress like a snake, climbing up my body, with the head coming to rest on my shoulder and dropping over my chest.

The Tanue. A different rendition than the one tattooed on Ravi's back, more primordial, but it was still beautiful. Something Mac had pointed out I shouldn't wear, considering that it was a symbol of the Krozalian Empire.

I was, essentially, still a Confederacy soldier. But the faux pas hadn't occurred to me while I'd been in Esme's shop going from dress to dress. Even Cassandra had whooped with awe and delight when she'd seen it, and Mac had refrained from pointing out anything until a few minutes ago when there was no time to back out.

"I'll get you for this," I'd promised when I'd gone to answer the knock at the door, vowing all sorts of retribution if I got in any trouble for it.

The look Ravi was giving me now wiped away all the doubts and made me stand taller.

"You look," he began, then shook his head. "Beautiful doesn't quite capture how stunning you look," he finished with a regal bow.

"So do you," I blurted and instantly blushed, feeling like an inexperienced teenager.

I ignored Mac's snicker and placed my hand in the crook of Ravi's extended elbow. His skin was hot and slick, and my fingers flexed involuntarily.

"Where's the ritual taking place?" I asked, half-expecting to be taken into the wilderness of Krozalia, somewhere high, overlooking the sea.

Instead, Ravi led me into a small alcove at the end of a large corridor that I'd thought was purely decorative. Though the ones I'd passed before held statues or pedestals or some ornament, this alcove stood empty.

We moved into the small space, and I looked for a

disguised latch that would open a hidden passage. Given the rotating seating arrangement in my room, it wasn't a farfetched assumption. Besides, in this sprawling castle with shifting walls, it was a marvel people didn't get lost more often. Or maybe they did. Cassandra and Sullivan had already confessed to that.

Ravi didn't disappoint. He touched the light fixture and a zing of static sparked. It wasn't big, but strong enough that even I felt it.

"So, that's how," Mac murmured. We'd spent the best part of the night scouring for the latch that would spin the wall in the bedroom, to no avail. Because magic was needed.

The ground under my feet gave a distant rumble, and the alcove began rotating. I shifted for better balance, and Ravi's hot hands clamped onto my elbows.

I peered up and smiled.

In response, he pulled me closer, his arms encircling me as his lips brushed my forehead.

"I'm sorry I didn't mention the dress code when I invited you last night."

"Why didn't you?"

"I didn't think you needed it," he said simply. "I don't need you to conform to our traditions; I accept you just the way you are. But then Zafra explained I'd have embarrassed you in front of everyone and that some might even have taken offense." His arms tightened before relaxing again. "I apologize for that."

I searched his face, finding nothing but telltale signs of exhaustion. I cupped his cheek, then speared my fingers through his hair and over the back of his head. I only needed a small pressure to bring his mouth closer. The kiss was slow and tender and all too brief.

"Apology accepted," I murmured against his lips.

Ravi sighed and touched his forehead to mine. From this close, the colors of his eyes seemed to move around like star specks in the twilight sky. I let myself get a bit lost in the shifting colors, just breathing him in.

"Why shirtless?" I asked.

He dropped his arms, took a step back, and turned around. His tattoo seemed bigger and alive, more dragon-like and feral than the rendition on my dress. His tribal tattoo on his neck—snaking lines and an infinity circle—looked like a twisted crown atop the creature's head, giving it a regal air.

"This is a ritual that involves the Tanue," he explained as he turned back to face me. "Everyone present will be honoring it—a tattoo, embroidery, or headset." He reached for my hand and entwined our fingers, something I'd never done with anyone else.

It felt good. It felt right.

"Let's go. We don't want to be late."

Where there'd been an alcove, was now a corridor. It stretched to both sides, identical to the one we'd just left. Not a secret passage, not another room, but another elegant hallway with tapestries and decorative statues and plush carpets.

"I wonder if this is the royal wing," Mac mused.

"Where are we going?" I asked.

"To the Ancestry's Hall."

"Hmm." It wasn't like I knew the castle's layout, even if he told me we were going somewhere else. I followed him around the bend and straight to the shiny purple door at the end. The closer we got to it, the more nervous I became, until my skin was crawling.

I stopped a few meters away and pulled my hand from Ravi's. "What's that?" I asked, crossing my arms over my chest.

Ravi looked from me to the door and back again. "You can feel it?"

I tore my gaze away from the door and glanced at him. "Shouldn't I?"

"I don't know." He touched a finger to the door and looked down at me. "This is fifty percent KKM."

"Why is it here?" I asked.

"It amplifies the ward on the lift. Only someone with clearance can come through."

The door parted, revealing a small room, empty of

furniture or decoration. I opened my mouth, then shut it again with a frown. "You said lift?"

Ravi stepped in, and I followed suit. "Yes."

The door behind me slid shut and set my teeth on edge. That familiar rumbling came again when we began moving. But instead of going up, we began to go down. Down and down and down. The only sign we were still moving was the vibration of the gears underneath the soles of my shoes. It went on long enough that the walls seemed to be shrinking, closing me in.

Claustrophobia had never been an issue. But in that square box hurtling down to an unknown location, the phobia started creeping in. Like small tendrils entwining around my neck and slowly cutting off my oxygen.

I was about to ask Ravi if there was another way to reach the Ancestry's Hall when the lift came to a smooth stop. It opened to a brightly lit stone hallway that exuded smells of anise and sage, and night-blooming jasmine. There were also no traces of KKM. Combined with the large space ahead and the brightness, a modicum of relief started spreading inside me.

"Where are we?" I asked again.

"In the bowels of the castle," Ravi replied quietly. "A hundred meters below the shoreline."

We'd certainly gone far enough that I wouldn't have batted an eyelash if he told me we'd gone farther than that. We stepped out of the lift together, our footsteps echoing faintly.

"This place is considered the tomb of the royal family," he murmured as we rounded a corner. "It's also where every Kroz who dies in service is buried. My crew died defending the princess, and although their bodies were lost in space, we will honor their spirits."

We followed the meandering passage as he continued. It was the first time he'd spoken about his crew, and I listened without interrupting.

"I lost ten men and women that day, and today, their closest families will come to say goodbye and return their essence to the void."

"They won't mind my presence?" I asked, aware that by his explanation, I'd be the only outsider in the crowd.

"No."

But the moment we entered the biggest cavern I'd ever seen, everyone turned to look at us—at me. And there were at least three dozen Kroz present. All the men were dressed similarly to Ravi, their torso and backs gleaming with oil, their tattoos on display. Not everyone's tattoo was as big as Ravi's, or even on their backs. Some had theirs on their biceps, others on their chests, or necks. There was even one with a scalp tattoo like Evo's.

I found Dolenta and Emperor Rokoskiv to the side with a small group that included Zafra, Furox, and three other Kroz: Lorvel and Ozvie, and a woman that looked a lot like Furox.

Dolenta gave me a smile and a wave, and I smiled back. I didn't return the wave because it didn't feel appropriate; not with everyone's attention on me.

With his hand on my lower back, Ravi guided me to where the Emperor stood. I wasn't sure if I was better off standing with them, or if I should have been taken to the bigger group. I, the outsider, in the presence of the elite.

My eyes fell on Ozvie and stuck there for a moment.

"He doesn't look old enough," Mac observed.

It was the same thought I'd had. Ozvie looked like Ravi's older brother, but not his father. But then again, Ravi had said his parents had been mated for three centuries. The life-mate bond was working in their favor.

I scanned the rest of the group, recognizing a few faces too. Not all the women wore black, or a dress. But as Ravi had explained and from what I could see, everyone had embroidery of the Tanue in their outfits.

"Relax," Ravi murmured.

Mac scoffed. "Easy to say when he isn't the party-crasher and everyone's center of focus."

True. But it didn't mean Ravi was wrong. Everyone's attention was on me, and I was stiff and nervous for all to see.

I took a deep breath, relaxed my stance, and put on my amiable mask. I stepped beside Ravi and mimicked him, bowing to the emperor when he did.

"Your majesty," he murmured, then he turned to his parents. "Father. Mother." He lowered his chin in acknowledgment to each. Then he turned to the other woman. "Vroja Milva."

Vroja. I remembered that word: aunt. She didn't look as young as Lorvel, but she still didn't look old enough to be Furox's mother. But the resemblance between them was striking.

I clasped my hands together behind my back and said nothing. If I'd known the memorial ritual was an exclusive event for such a tight-knit group, I'd have declined the invitation. But I was here now, and I wasn't going to make a fool of myself by trying to impress anyone.

Ravi's hand fell on my shoulder and squeezed. "I believe you've already met Leann," he said to his parents. "I am courting her."

Silence fell in the large cavern. It hadn't been too noisy to begin with, but Ravi's declaration fell like a bombshell.

It was the aunt, Milva, who broke the ice. "Finally," she said with a smile aimed at Ravi and me. "Some positive news."

Someone in the larger group chuckled. Milva reached for me with both hands and pulled me in for a fragrant hug. She had on a beige jumpsuit embroidered with the Tanue climbing up her right leg, circling her back, and resting its head on her belly.

Milva let me go, only for Lorvel to do the same, embracing me and kissing both my cheeks. She had on a ruby-red three-piece suit, with a smaller design of the Tanue, which I assumed was mostly on her back, given only the claws and the tail showed in the front.

Ozvie only gave me a friendly wink and turned to address the crowd. "Today, we mourn our dead. Tomorrow, we celebrate my son's life-mate bond."

I startled at the announcement and turned to Ravi. I hadn't consented to the bond, much less to any celebration in honor of it.

His expression was blank as he lowered his head and kissed my cheek. "I'll talk to him," he murmured near my ear.

"You better."

My eyes locked with Lorvel's assessing gaze. There wasn't any animosity there, but I couldn't discern any joy either.

"We will begin," the emperor announced.

As one, the assembled Kroz turned and spread into one line, facing the back of the cavern—that was a lot of naked backs and tattoos in varying shapes and sizes. I could also see the tribal tattoos of most, save for some of the women who had their hair down. Going by the different symbols, there were only three tribes present here, unless I counted the emperor's, which was a series of slashes and dashes in a pattern I couldn't identify. Dolenta was the only one present without a tribal tattoo, but I knew it was only because she had yet to reach her majority.

Emperor Rokoskiv motioned, and Ravi gave my shoulder another reassuring squeeze, and stepped to his side. I ended up between Milva on my right and Lorvel on my left.

When I faced forward like everyone else, I realized that the space wasn't dim because the Kroz only bothered to light half of it. No, the back of the cavern was dark because ten meters away, the ground dropped into a chasm that went as far as my eyes could see. And I could usually see far.

There was an air of expectation, and while everyone knew what was about to happen, I had no clue.

When holograph images of ten Kroz appeared by the lip of the chasm, I flinched. It wasn't every day that I climbed down into the bowels of a planet where the air was heavy with energy, everyone dressed for a theme, and people appeared out of nowhere. Granted, they were only images of the crew I assumed were killed on Ravi's ship, but still.

Lorvel angled closer as the emperor began speaking. In Krozalian, of course.

Why speak a language only one person needs? Besides, maybe the ritual was more symbolic than I'd thought, and speaking in Universal would have been construed as an insult to the dead.

Lorvel leaned close to my ear. I braced for some hateful words to spill from her mouth, my heart pounding with nervousness.

"He's commending the fallen warriors for their bravery and wishing them a peaceful passage."

I gave her a sideways look, then nodded my thanks. Lorvel straightened, her lips tilting at the corners, as if amused at how nervous she made me.

A teenage boy detached from the line and approached the holograph further on the right. He pulled a small bejeweled dagger from a side sheath around his waist and sliced the meatier part of his palm. Blood welled immediately, and he let it fall into a delicate urn a Kroz woman was holding.

Vera. I hadn't recognized her before. She was dressed in a similar dress to mine, only hers ended above her knee and was slit on both sides.

The teenaged Kroz circled his hand with a hankie and stepped back. Another Kroz stepped forward, this one older, with graying hair and laugh lines around his grief-stricken eyes. His dagger had carvings instead of jewels on the grip, but it looked just as ritualistic as the boy's had. He cut his palm the way the teenager did and let his blood spill into the urn.

"We usually return the body to the void," Lorvel murmured, "but when the body isn't available, the blood of a close relative is given instead."

Ah, that explained the bloodletting.

I was surprised when Dolenta stepped forward, accepted a gold-crusted blade from the emperor, and sliced her hand without flinching or hesitating. I watched as she let her blood flow into the urn, then wrapped her hand with a hankie the emperor offered her.

"Taleem was her uncle," Lorvel explained. "Her last remaining relative."

Vera raised the urn and everyone started singing, even the

emperor. I wanted to step back and leave, never having felt like an intruder as acutely as I felt then. I had no right to be there, witnessing and sharing the grief as if I belonged. I didn't.

Unbidden tears sprang to my eyes, coaxed forth by the haunting song even if I couldn't understand a word. Grief and longing built in the cavern as Vera approached the lip of the hole, cutting between the holographs without stirring or breaking the images.

Without warning, she threw the urn into the darkness exactly at the moment everyone stopped singing. I watched it sail into the air and disappear. I waited for it to reach the bottom. I never heard a thing.

Chapter 20

"The use of Kukona minerals shall be strictly prohibited for any military applications, including but not limited to nuclear components, ammunition, handguns, explosives, and bladed weaponry. It shall not be employed for the advancement of war machinery, such as atmospheric aircraft, stealth ships, or watercraft. Nor shall it be utilized in the development of sentient experiments, whether intended for domestic assistance, ecological research, space exploration, or deep space endeavors."

The negotiator went on with all the restrictions for which the Kukona minerals weren't allowed to be used, and Lorenzo sat, docilely listening, and occasionally nodding in agreement.

I was expecting him to snarl and go for the Kroz's throat any moment.

Any moment now…

Vera had come knocking an hour after Ravi had returned me to my room. He had promised to take me to dinner later, once he finished some of the things he had to oversee. The moment I'd seen the Kroz spy at my door, I recalled agreeing to undergo a physical examination. With all that had happened since, I'd managed to completely forget about it. But that hadn't been Vera's intention.

Not that I'd been thrilled when she'd announced the negotiations for KKM were underway and my presence had been requested.

Blech.

I sent Ravi a message, letting him know where I was going in the event he finished before I did, and followed Vera out. Lorenzo had glared at me for being late but hadn't given me any of his hostile attitude. On the contrary, his eyes were practically glowing with excitement. His proposal must have not been so bad, because there sat the Minister of Trade and a negotiator whose names I hadn't asked and hadn't been given.

The negotiator stopped speaking. I brought my attention back to the two Kroz patiently watching Lorenzo. "What say you, Commodore? Does the Confederacy agree to our terms?"

I half expected Lorenzo to scoff at the absurdity. There was no reason to make an agreement that the Confederacy wouldn't benefit from.

"The Human Confederacy agrees to your terms and conditions."

I almost fell off my chair with surprise.

"They must be desperate for it," Mac commented.

I agreed. To think that Lorenzo had just spoken for the entire Confederacy. I hadn't known he had that much authority. His mother, yes, but it was common knowledge that his mother didn't hold him in high regard. She had, after all, sent him to fight for the CTF when, as an Earth-born, his conscription was not compulsory. I'd expected him to discuss the terms and conditions with higher-ranking officials, then for another lengthy negotiation to ensue with the Kroz. I'd honestly expected the trade agreement to go back and forth for a few years before things were finalized.

"Very well," the negotiator said, pushing a thin tablet toward Lorenzo. "This is the agreement in written form. Sign and seal, and once payment is received, we'll start shipping to the agreed location."

Once Lorenzo and the negotiator signed, the Minister of Trade placed his seal and stood. Lorenzo and the rest of us did the same. The negotiator smiled, extended a hand, and said, "I hear your culture calls for a handshake when agreements are made."

Lorenzo grasped the hand and shook. "It's been an honor," he said. "Once we're back at Sector 8, we'll transfer payment."

The Minister of Trade nodded, glanced once at me, and turned to go, the negotiator in tow.

"I don't understand what you want with the KKM," I said once the door shut behind the Kroz. "Not after you practically agreed it can be used for nothing but pretty bobbles."

Lorenzo sat back and sighed. "I don't expect you to understand." The words weren't insulting, just tired, as if he too recognized the futility of the agreement.

"You know if you break faith, you'll be giving the Kroz an opening to attack?"

Lorenzo gave me a scathing look. "You don't know anything."

I opened my mouth and then shut it again. The Kroz negotiator had left, but Vera was still in the room, and although she was dressed in a server's uniform, I knew her position in the Kroz hierarchy wasn't so benevolent. I met her eyes and stood. It was time to go and let the Kroz examine and prod my insides. I moved past Lorenzo, bent, and whispered, "Don't be a fool. The Kroz has eyes everywhere."

I straightened and kept going, not looking back to ascertain if Lorenzo understood.

I found Ravi standing guard at the door, hands clasped behind his back. His eyes moved from where the negotiator was just disappearing around the corner and down at me, gaze inscrutable. "You done?"

I stepped aside for Vera to exit before responding. Leaving my back vulnerable made me uneasy, and knowing what I knew about Vera, leaving my back vulnerable to her made me twitchy. I offered Ravi an apologetic look. "I forgot when I agreed to dinner that I was to head out with Vera for the physical," I began just as Cassandra stuck her head out the door.

"Out?" she repeated. "You going to sightsee again? Can I come?"

"No." My reply was quick and wary.

Cassandra's eyes were shrewd as they darted from Vera to Ravi and back to me. "Why not? Lorenzo and Sullivan are deliberating the merits of leaving tomorrow or the day after. It's not like we have much longer on Krozalia."

"I-I have some things to see to."

"I heard. A physical," she said, scrutinizing me. "Are you sick?"

"No."

"Then I want to come. We were assured we're not prisoners here." She aimed the latter at Ravi. "I was told we could leave the castle and explore any time we wished to. We're all going to go and celebrate the start of a new alliance. If you need to go somewhere before that, I'll come with you. There's no reason why you should miss on the fun."

"That sounds like a good idea," Ravi said before Vera or I could speak, not that Vera looked like she was going to intervene, standing there patiently waiting. "We'll all celebrate."

Cassandra beamed and gave him two thumbs up. "Awesome. I'll just grab my shoes and we can go." She rushed back in, leaving the door open.

Vera raised an eyebrow at me. I sighed.

"It's not like I'd rather be poked and prodded instead of having fun," I said to Ravi, "but I did promise the emperor."

"I already spoke with the emperor," he said to Vera. "I'll bring Leann to Doctor Lamis later tonight."

It was a sign of Ravi's influence that Vera didn't question him further. But then again, if Ravi was lying, Vera could easily find out, and the lie would damage whatever good standing Ravi had with the emperor.

Vera gave Ravi a curt nod and melted away, her passage silent.

"Do you think that she'd mind?" I asked. That was the kind of woman I didn't want to have as an enemy. Patient, quiet, and dangerous. Qualities of an efficient hunter.

"People who usually spend time with those three either leave in tears or in a body bag," Furox had said.

"He ranks higher," Mac observed. "Maybe even right under the emperor himself."

It was true. When Emperor Rokoskiv had been in the room and Ravi had told Vera to sit, she'd waited for the emperor's approval, but here, without the emperor, he had the authority to tell her what to do. It was a good thing to know. Not that I had any reason to use that, because I wouldn't.

"No. She no longer considers you a threat to the emperor, so it doesn't matter to her either way."

We watched as she disappeared around the corner. I exhaled and leaned against the wall beside Ravi. I had agreed to the physical, but it didn't mean I was looking forward to it.

Ravi pulled me to him and I went willingly, dropping my forehead on his shoulder and breathing in his spicy scent. His arms went around my waist, his cheek on the top of my head. "I'm sorry you have to go through this." His arms squeezed me tight, then loosened.

I looked up and met the umber of his eyes a second before his mouth covered mine. Raw, unfiltered desire electrified my nerves, bringing everything to life. My hands moved up his chest and around his neck, while his arms squeezed me against the hard edges of his body.

We broke the kiss when Cassandra shouted something from inside the suite.

"You do things to me," he murmured against my lips, then pulled back when footsteps approached fast.

I put some space between us in time for Cassandra to explode out of the room, followed by Sullivan and Lorenzo. Her eyes, hard and battle-ready, scanned the corridor, then swiveled back to me. "What's up with that maid?" She shivered once. "She gives me the creeps, standing there watching us like a meat-pecker scouring for her next meal." She slanted Ravi a sideways glance. "No offense."

"None taken."

Cassandra gave me an assessing look and looped her arm around mine. "Lord Drax, do you mind going ahead? I'd like a word with Leann."

Ravi squeezed my shoulder and strolled after Sullivan

and Lorenzo.

I gave Cassandra a quizzical look. "What is it?"

"I just wanted to make sure you're okay." She leaned close to my ear and said, "Are you in trouble with the Kroz?" Her eyes bore into mine when she leaned back, filled with concern.

I tilted my head to the side, trying to figure out what exactly she was trying to get at.

"Sunny and I had a talk earlier about a few things," she said knowingly, no doubt catching the question in my expression.

"The bastard is gambling with your life," Mac snarled, his voice laced with anger.

It took me a few seconds to fully comprehend the meaning of her words, and even then, it was Mac's comment that drove it in. I jerked and glared at Sullivan's back. *The fucker.*

"He told you."

Cassandra squeezed my arm. "We're good," she assured me. "Nothing changed."

My heart pounded painfully in my neck as I processed her words. Her eyes were soft and warm, and the understanding in them almost undid me. "I can't convince Lorenzo that we should make a run for it because a lot is hanging on this trade going through, but if you need me to be there for this physical you mentioned earlier, I'll come with you. Losing you and Alex almost killed me once. I'm not going to stand by now that I have you back. For better or worse, I'm going to be there for you."

Tears pricked my eyes, but I refused to let them fall. Not because I didn't want to feel, but because I refused to celebrate with puffy eyes.

I pulled Cassandra in for a hug, squeezing gently. "Thank you."

She held me back tightly. "I'm not going to let anything happen to you," she promised, then stepped back and threw one arm around my shoulders. "Now, let's go party, baby."

We caught up with Ravi by the entrance. The others had

already disappeared from sight, but their voices could be heard from the left. "We're going to the Flying Crown," she told Ravi. "We'd love if you could join us."

Ravi's eyes glinted with mischief. "I wouldn't miss it."

Cassandra let me go, winked, and hurried after Sullivan and Lorenzo. We watched until she disappeared from view as well.

Ravi's hand slipped into mine and squeezed. "Let's go," he said.

I looked back. "You don't mind that, do you? We can still go somewhere else. Cassie will understand."

"I was already taking you to the Flying Crown."

It was the way he spoke that had me giving him a sideways look. "Is something about to happen?"

Ravi looked down at me and smiled, eyes crinkling at the corners. "You'll see."

Chapter 21

There was a unique identifier to taverns no matter their location. The bar, the sitting arrangements, even the ruckus laughter and loud conversations. They were present regardless of which planet, station, or sector I found myself in.

The Flying Crown was no different. It was loud, it was full, and it smelled of alcohol and cooking food.

Sullivan and Lorenzo peeled towards the bar the moment we stepped in. "We'll order," Sullivan called over his shoulder. "First round is on Lorenzo."

Lorenzo snorted and kept going, not complaining or denying Sullivan's claim.

"He must be in a really good mood," I muttered. "I don't remember ever seeing him so…mellow."

Cassandra laughed. "He's ecstatic. No one's ever been able to brokerage this type of deal. Lorenzo is looking at a nice recognition award and status elevation after this. And it's all thanks to you." She thumped me twice on the back.

We watched the two walk away until they were swallowed by the crowd. Then Ravi led us to the back where we'd eaten breakfast earlier, where the tables were reserved for special guests. To my surprise, we found Zafra and none other than the emperor and Dolenta already there. There were also other warriors, scattered in the room dressed like civilians. The only reason I knew they were warriors was because I'd seen them earlier in the Ancestry's Hall. Even Zafra had on a floral dress, white and yellow with blue trimmings at the hem. It was the first time I'd seen her out of the Kroz armor. At the far corner, my eyes snagged on Furox's spiky red hair. He sat with a brunette Kroz, dressed in a white long-sleeve tunic that gave him a ruddy complexion. Their heads were bent together and it took me a while to recognize the bundle he held for what it was: his son.

I took a step his way just as someone shouted and diverted my attention.

Dolenta waved enthusiastically when I glanced her way. "Leann! Leann, Captain Lee. Over here."

I detoured in her direction, Cassandra and Ravi flanking me. Some of the disguised warriors glanced at us, noted Ravi, and looked away. I assumed that was the green go-ahead. Dolenta hugged me when we reached her, then hugged Cassandra. She touched a hand to Ravi's, and the warmth in his eyes told me the show of affection was new and welcomed.

"Sit with us," Dolenta invited us.

I glanced at the emperor, but he said nothing, content to just sit and watch his daughter over a cup of steaming tea. "We don't want to intrude," I began, unsure what the protocol was. Ravi was certainly expected to join them, and maybe by default, so was I, but I didn't think the emperor was open to sharing his table with the Human Confederacy. Even if he did, his people wouldn't. If for no other reason than it could be construed as a security breach.

"We'll take this one." Ravi pulled the chair closest to the emperor's table for me. "You can table-hop and gossip too," he told the princess.

Dolenta's solemn look turned into a radiant smile. She grabbed the chair Ravi had pulled for me and sat. Before Ravi could pull the next chair for me, I grabbed the chair to Dolenta's other side and sat. "Go," I told him. "We need a girl's moment here."

Dolenta's eyes sparkled. Ravi dropped a peck on my mouth and assumed Dolenta's previous seat with the emperor.

"How're you settling?" Cassandra asked. "Has your schooling resumed?"

Dolenta scowled. "I'm only allowed to have strategy

classes. Papa doesn't want the educators in the royal wing and I'm not allowed to leave it without the six."

The six being her guard entourage. I could see the curiosity Dolenta's words sparked, and before Cassandra could give them voice, I changed the topic. "It'll all be over soon. I'll ask Ravi if you can have lunch with us tomorrow."

"Yes." Cassandra clapped. "It'll be like a goodbye luncheon for old time's sake."

Dolenta's head whipped around. Hurt purple eyes searched my face. "You're leaving?"

"The day after tomorrow," Lorenzo said as he pulled the chair next to Cassandra.

Sullivan lowered the tray onto our table and claimed the seat between Cassandra and me. "Don't be crestfallen, kiddo," Sullivan said. "I bet the captain will return as soon as she can." He began distributing glasses filled with silver liquid around.

I touched Dolenta's hand but didn't say anything. I didn't know what to say. I hadn't agreed to leave, but I needed to go, if for no other reason than I needed to undo the CTF's hold over me. It was past time I resumed my search for Alex. I had already delayed long enough with this trip, even though I hadn't expected to leave so soon. But I knew I'd be going.

Ravi appeared to Dolenta's other side and sat, accepting a silver-filled glass from Sullivan. He winked, raised the drink, and took a sip. Shards of glass sliced my heart at the knowledge that our time together was coming to an end. For a moment, a crazy moment, I wondered if I should give up looking for Alex. Baltsar had told me, time and again, that we hadn't left anyone living in the facility and that even if Alex had survived and been relocated, he could be anywhere in the galaxy. *Maybe it was time to let go and start living for myself.*

The gnawing longing that thought conjured was so strong, my eyes stung with tears. I lowered my head and waited until the moment passed. Had the roles been reversed, I knew Alex would have never stopped searching for me. Not until he found me, or conclusive evidence that I was dead.

Dolenta laughed at something Sullivan said. I looked up, my eyes locking on Ravi's penetrating gaze. He lowered his drink, eyebrows knitting, as if he could read my disturbing thoughts. Maybe he could. Not literally, but he'd certainly proven that he could read me better than anyone else I knew.

My throat tightened. Maybe leaving the day after tomorrow was a good thing. Not that it felt like it at the moment. My insides were knotting and twisting with pain, but prolonging my stay would only complicate things. For me, for Mac, and Ravi. We were never going to work out, no matter what.

Maybe I wasn't a hypermorph, but Mac was a sentient AI, and that was a line the emperor wouldn't overlook. There was a chance Ravi would accept that Mac was part of my life, but no one else would be as understanding. I had no trouble lying to people, but myself was a different matter.

Ravi's kisses took my breath away and made me forget my objectives, but I had no right in promising him a chance when I knew that wasn't going to happen. Strangely, the revelation only intensified the ache inside me.

"Is it true?" Dolenta asked me.

I brought my attention back to the table. Everyone was looking at me.

"We've always said that if the military didn't work," Cassandra was saying, "she could always try her hand at singing."

"What?" I choked on the sip I'd taken of the silver drink.

"Cassandra said you're a talented singer," Dolenta explained once I stopped coughing.

"She could have won awards," Sullivan avowed.

"I like to sing," I said succinctly. "That doesn't make me a singer."

"Not everyone can sing," Sullivan said and shuddered. "Some people just make noise."

A fist-sized pretzel hit him on the face and Dolenta giggled.

"My noises are rhythmic," Cassandra objected haughtily.

Imperial Stardust

"At least I can carry a tune."

Sullivan dropped the pretzel on the table and licked crumbs off his fingers. "I never said I could sing. You were the one who insisted I try."

"Whatever," she flicked a dismissive finger and turned her attention on to me. "Now, I promised the kid you'd give her a show."

"What?" I squeaked. "Now? Here? What are you drinking?"

"Something good that you'll miss out on when Sullivan finishes his and grabs yours." She raised her half glass and directed it toward Ravi. "Ask your man. Best. Drink. Ever."

"So it is," he confirmed, leaning back, his glass in one hand as he watched the exchange with amused eyes.

"Come on," Sullivan cajoled. "You know you want it."

"Yeah," Cassandra sing-songed. "You live for it."

I snorted, but I couldn't hold my glower before I started smiling.

"Please," Dolenta added.

Before I could agree or disagree, a sharp clap rang out from my right and a hush descended upon the crowd. "Attention, please," a gruff voice called—and not for the first time.

The mood in the tavern went from loudly cheerful to tension-filled silence.

"What's going on?" I asked.

Dolenta squirmed beside me. "The announcement," she whispered. "My father broadcast earlier that he would make an announcement regarding the situation in Krozalia."

I glanced back at the emperor, but he was just sitting there, looking…defeated. I opened my mouth to ask more, but Dolenta stood and went to sit with her father, dropping her small hand over his in obvious comfort. The look of defeat was wiped off his face, but he remained seated, showing no intention of delivering a speech. My question was answered a moment later when I followed everyone's gaze to a long holographic view of the Tanue, dominating the entire east wall of the tavern. This one was black and amethyst and looked more like the dragon the creature reminded me of. It snaked around in a sinewy dance, twisting and turning without pause.

The Tanue disappeared, replaced by a holographic recording of the emperor. He was in a vast chamber with high, vaulted ceilings, flanked by his advisors, along with Ravi's parents—and Dolenta. They were still dressed in the clothes from the memorial ritual, so it had either been recorded before or after. I suspected after, and that those were the items Ravi told me he had to oversee earlier.

"People of Krozalia," the emperor began. "I have been a servant of the crown for the past ten decades without fault. I've ruled with hope and faith and fairness. I've led you into more prosperity than my forebearers. I have bled and cried and laughed for you. I have united Krozalians into one.

"Unlike other mystical races, we are uniquely capable of guiding the energy the Tanue bestowed upon us. We have searched many planets, ventured into unchartered parts of the galaxy, seeking others like us without success. Although some races have the aptitude to cast magic, they still pale in comparison, lacking the Ashak and the control needed to wield energy at will. The Kroz are unique in that aspect, yet we're no better than any other race.

"My predecessors decided that Krozalia was the key, and so we opened our gates to other races, regardless of their magical strengths. Yet no one has developed the ability to commune with the Tanue. That affinity remains exclusive to the Kroz, particularly to the royal family. Despite that, some of you have deemed me unfit to rule and have tried multiple assassination attempts in the past few years.

"I've given no mercy for those who've plotted against the crown. In the past years, we've sundered more Kroz than we have in the past century."

An image of the execution from yesterday replaced the recording of the emperor, the moment when Ravi swept his arms to both sides and made all the traitors disappear. Then came other sundering from other times, all playing in quick succession.

"So many," Mac murmured.

The holograph of the emperor and the advisors appeared again. "I am a servant of the crown," he said, inhaling a deep breath. "But my people are discontent with my rule. This unsettles the Tanue, and when the balance is lost, Krozalia suffers. Plagues have begun in the east, while the west faces floods and avalanches. The north and south are seeing an increase in volcanic eruptions and drought. My citizens have taken to the streets to riot and cause mayhem. It is for that reason that today, I, Rokoskiv Tsakid the Fourth, formally relinquish monarchical authority."

I jolted with shock. Cassandra gasped. Sullivan cursed softly. Yet no one else in the tavern said or did anything.

In the holograph, the emperor stepped back and pulled the crown from his head.

"Tomorrow, my heir, Dolenta Tsakid, will be crowned Empress of Krozalia. For the next decade, I'll serve as regent until she's old enough to rule on her own. May she reign with kindness and faith and fairness." The emperor went down to one knee and all the advisors did the same. "All hail your next empress."

Everyone in the tavern slipped from their seats and went down to their knees. I followed suit. Only Dolenta remained seated, hands clasped in her lap and a look of pure misery in her eyes.

Zafra was the first to clap. Soon, everyone in the tavern, including the Kroz warriors and the emperor, started clapping until the sound turned thunderous. Dolenta's cheeks went red and she offered a wobbly smile.

"We'll celebrate!" Cassandra shouted.

Another round of applause went up, broken by Sullivan's piercing whistles. But all went silent when the emperor stood. "I'll cut my stay short," he stated. "Please, continue your celebration." Dolenta followed suit, and the emperor put a hand on her shoulder and kissed her cheek. "Stay with your friends."

He nodded at Zafra and made his way to the back, where a discreet door half hidden by a decorative pillar, stood.

"Wait for me," Ravi told me as he followed the emperor out, along with half of the warriors.

Zafra took Ravi's seat, pushing his empty glass away and placing hers in its place. Cassandra pulled out her commlink and beckoned Dolenta closer. "My brother is going to foam at the mouth with jealousy when I tell him I'm friends with the empress."

Dolenta flashed her a shy smile, but there was sadness in her eyes too.

"Come closer," Cassandra instructed, setting her commlink to hover above the table in front of them.

Zafra plucked it from the air. "You pose; I'll take the photo."

Cassandra crouched behind Dolenta's chair and Zafra snapped the photo.

"Now you, Leann, come closer."

I leaned sideways and put an arm around Dolenta's shoulders. "Besties forever," Cassandra declared.

We repeated along. Then Zafra handed Lorenzo the commlink so she could join us, then Furox was there, and Sullivan. By the time we were done, Cassandra had taken dozens of photos and we were on our third drink.

"Time to pay the piper," Cassandra told me with a wicked grin. "Show us that killer voice."

"Forget it," I told her. "I'm not going to sing in a crowded tavern."

"Come on, Clara," she pleaded. "You've never been shy of karaoke before." She clasped both hands together, elbowed Dolenta, and whispered loud enough to wake the dead, "Follow my lead."

Dolenta clasped her hands together, and echoed Cassandra's "Pleaaaase."

"You're a bad influence," I told her. "The empress should never beg for anything she wants."

Imperial Stardust

"Agreed," Zafra said, eyes gleaming with amusement. "She orders, and you obey."

"And the empress has given her first order: sing!" Cassandra punctuated the statement with a slap to the tabletop.

It was the sad puppy-dog look in Dolenta's eyes that made me relent. I sighed. "Just this once."

Cassandra did a little dance—elbow jabbing, hips swinging. Sullivan let out a two-finger whistle that made my eardrums vibrate.

"One song," I warned. "Nothing more."

"We'll bass for you," Cassandra said, sliding into the chair across from mine. She thumped her fists on the top of the table, clapped, then thumped again.

Sullivan picked up the rhythm, clapping twice, then thumping his fists. To our left, Zafra and Furox picked up the beat too.

I recognized the beat: "Forgotten Hero", a song that had gone viral in the year I'd joined the Confederacy. It was a haunting ballad about an unloved child who joined the military to prove to everyone that he was someone worthy of their notice. He rose through the ranks swiftly, only to die protecting the village where no one remembered him.

It was a poignant song, a duet that I used to sing with Alex by my side. For a moment, I debated telling them that I'd changed my mind, but the gleam of anticipation in Dolenta's purple eyes told me to suck it up.

So, I sang.

Dolenta picked up the clapping and thumping, and before I closed my eyes, I noticed that the tavern had gone quiet, save for the rhythmic thump and clap.

Clap clap, thump. Clap clap, thump. Clap, thump, clap. Clap clap, thump. Clap clap, thump. Clap, thump, clap.

When I reached the chorus, Cassandra sang the part Alex used to. The air whooshed out of me as if I'd been sucker-punched. From the glimmer of tears in her eyes, I realized she wasn't as unaffected by the memory as I'd thought. I stopped singing. Dolenta stopped clapping, and after a beat, so did everyone else. The silence that fell was deafening.

"Leann—" Sullivan began.

I stood. "I'll get the next round," I said huskily and hurried to the bar.

Chapter 22

I rushed into the tavern's bustling main room, feeling everyone's eyes on me, my back prickling beneath the weight of their scrutiny.

"What?" Mac asked. "What was that?"

"Nothing," I replied and gave the counter a light thump, though I didn't have to. The bartender was already making his way over.

"What can I get you?" he asked in heavily accented Universal.

"Another round of that silver drink for the Confederacy table and whatever chai you have available."

"Bitter or sweet?"

"Bitter," I decided. It was a bitter kind of moment.

"Well, if you don't want to talk about what has you in an obvious tizzy, I should tell you that I think I've cracked the Gamat Com firewall."

"Oh? Is that what you've been so preoccupied with?" I turned around to survey the rest of the tavern.

Laughter and animated conversations filled the air, and drinks flowed freely. It seemed like the emperor's announcement had lifted the people's spirits. Maybe there was more to the rebellion than simply wanting to replace the current regime. I recalled the emperor's talk about natural disasters and wondered if Thern had been trying to do the right thing. Not that I thought killing the princess or the emperor was the right course of action, but maybe something needed to be done. Maybe if he'd gone about it in a different way, things wouldn't have taken a drastic turn.

"Before you get all righteous, I should tell you that I was extra careful. If I found something I wasn't a hundred percent sure I could access, I didn't risk it. Not even for a ninety-nine percent chance."

I mulled that over. I had drawn that line because I was afraid of the consequences if he got caught. Yet, if Mac could guarantee his safety, then it was fucking worth it.

"What did you find?"

"Sadly, not as much as I wanted. I was only able to get through the surface shield."

I relaxed. Mac's frustration rang loud and clear. If in all this time, all he had managed was to crack a surface shield, then Mac was taking my warning seriously enough.

"There are so many branches, including the mainframe of several planets in every Sector. Leo was right. If he gets access to this, it'll be much easier for us to trace the scientists' movement."

"Here you go," the bartender said, placing the tray with my order in front of me. "On the house," he added when I reached to pay.

"Thanks." I grabbed the tray and returned to the back room.

I didn't engage in any of the talks going about, simply sipped my bitter chai quietly as I listened to the list of information hidden underneath another firewall shield Mac was trying to crack.

"Finances, import and export, agricultural gross value for consumers, and taxpayers for Sectors 6, 7, and 8. The viable plants used for medicine, drugs, and poisons within those same sectors. The incomings and outgoings of space stations of Sector 3 and 4, along with the export of several goods and weapons. The Kroz have their fingers on every pulse in the galaxy. But the most important thing I'm seeing is the KKM exports that leave Krozalia every quarter. I can't get into those files yet, but statistics tell me that with our current information, if we pursue those, we'll eventually be able to trace the scientists' movements."

It was a new perspective, more focused than the one we'd followed in all those years.

If the emperor was right and they could lock on to which KKM mine the ones used for my prosthetics came from and which batch, we might even be able to find the scientists' backers.

When Zafra indicated it was time for Dolenta to head back, I said my goodbyes and excused myself as well. The night outside wasn't hot, per se, but it was warmer than the tavern.

I took the right and walked fast, the sounds of other Kroz celebrating coming from all around. Fireworks and aircraft were everywhere—behind, in front, above.

I didn't have a destination in mind, so I just walked, trying to find a quiet corner. Mac was silent again, no doubt pouring over the wealth of information he could access. He'd examine them with a fine-tooth comb before he tried delving any deeper, and I knew that would keep him distracted.

I ventured into a copse of trees to avoid some of the crowd. My night vision allowed me to navigate through the tall trees, sprawling roots, and ditches without any incidents. I came to a stop sometime later by a low wall overlooking the black sea. I could hear the waves, see the white foam of the water smashing against the rocks, feel the increased humidity. The night sky was as breathtaking from here as it was from my balcony, streaked with starlight and the two hanging moons.

The sounds of revelry were muffled by the rustling of the trees behind me and the rocky seawall below. It allowed me to unwind and empty my mind of thoughts. Gradually, I released all my jumbled thoughts, until I was nothing but an empty cask tethered by my shell.

I wasn't sure how long I stood there, but when footsteps sounded behind me, I realized I'd been gone for a long time. I stepped to the side, closer to one of the trees, but I didn't have to.

"Leann?" Ravi called softly. "It's me."

My tension eased, but I didn't step away from my hiding

spot. He came into the open, his footsteps soft as if he was gliding atop the leaves and twigs, his countenance cloaked in shadows.

"You didn't have to come," I said when he propped his elbows on the low wall and waited for me.

He angled his head in my direction but kept his eyes on the water below. "I wanted to."

I wanted to ask him why but didn't. There was no need for us to dance this dance. I was leaving; he was staying. The time for a heart-to-heart discussion had passed. Maybe it had never come, but it certainly wasn't here or now.

"Lorenzo wants to leave the day after tomorrow," I began. "Can you provide him with an escort?"

Ravi turned then, looking straight at me, though his eyes were a bit unfocused. "Let me see you."

"No. Can you provide him with an escort?"

"You want to stay?" A hopeful inflection tinged the end of that sentence, a sentiment I wished I could disregard.

"I-I can't."

"Why?"

Why? One small word laden with a world of explanation and emotions. I could tell him it was none of his business. I could tell him I decided to return to duty. I could tell him so many things, and I considered them all and discarded them even faster. I inhaled and told him something I hadn't planned to. "I've been hunting for the scientists and their facilities for years. Aside from a crimp in their operations, I've made no difference. Now, I know about the KKM. I'd never had this advantage before."

Ravi was quiet for a long time, his hair fluttering like shadowy coils around his head. "You struck me once as a woman with a purpose, someone who'd do anything in her power to reach her goals. When Thern...that day on the bridge, I let myself believe that I was wrong, that you were just a woman with a deadly secret intent on surviving." He turned back to me and took a step closer. "But I was right the first time. You're going for the people that did this to you. Is it revenge or is it something else?"

I clamped my lips shut, then found myself answering. I'd told him the important parts; there was no reason to hold this one back. He deserved an honest answer, if nothing else. "Both."

"I've had some time to think about what happened to you and how you've been living since. They have your friend, don't they? Alex, the co-pilot. Is he a hypermorph?"

I started to deny it, then hesitated. "I don't know."

"You need to know so you can move on." It was a statement, not a question, and because it was spot on, I didn't say anything. I couldn't stay with him and couldn't go back to the Confederacy because both would hinder my search for the people responsible. And we both knew this wouldn't be a short run from sector to sector. It could be months before I found the culprits; it could be years. I couldn't make any commitments that would divert me from my goal. I owed this to Alex; I owed it to myself. I owed it to Ravi because he could still find someone else compatible, another mate-match more suitable than someone who was neither human nor hypermorph.

Ravi exhaled a harsh breath, no doubt coming to the same conclusion. He squeezed the back of his neck and then rubbed his palm over his face. "You've made up your mind."

"Yes."

"We should go see Doctor Lamis, the KKM expert. I promised the emperor I'd take you there tonight."

Regret and disappointment stabbed at me. This was for the best. It was what I'd wanted. I repeated that to myself as I finally stepped away from the tree.

To my surprise, there was no transport waiting for us. The celebration was still going strong in some parts of the town, but it was obviously slowing down.

Ravi led me through side streets until we reached the road back to the castle, the lights of the town behind and the lights of the castle ahead casting the road into darkness. "Are we walking to the castle?" I asked, unable to hold in my curiosity. It wasn't a great distance, but at this time and in this darkness, there wasn't any scenic view to enjoy.

"No, just up ahead," Ravi replied.

A few meters later, we came to a side road that was more of a gap in the foliage, half-hidden by all the trees. Had it not been for Ravi, I would have never noticed it—I hadn't noticed it before, and I'd come up and down this road a few times now. It was narrow and lined with trees on both sides, like the road to a private residence.

Ravi trundled a few steps ahead of me as if he couldn't bear to walk by my side. As if he wanted to get me to my destination so he could leave. I realized then and there that he deserved more from me, that I needed to make this right, even if we'd soon be going our separate ways. *The time for a heart-to-heart confession may be behind us, but it didn't have to be.*

"Ravi," I said and waited for him to stop. "I want you to know that I would stay had the situation been different."

He turned to me, eyes unreadable in the shadows. "If I promised to put my best on this case? You know this isn't something the Kroz is going to ignore."

I stepped closer. Emotion flickered in his eyes, but I still couldn't read it. I closed the gap, brushed my knuckles against his prickly stubble, and searched his eyes. "Would you, if you were in my place, delegate a cause this important to your heart to someone else?"

A blank mask fell over his face, shutting me out completely. I raised on tiptoes and brushed my mouth against his unresponsive lips.

"I am sorry, Ravi." I kept my grip firm on his arm when he made to step back. "I'd love to spend my life by your side. I want to wake up next to you every morning and go to bed with you every night. You make me whole in a way I've never in my life been, and I want nothing but to abandon all and stay. But I can't. Not when I know what happens in those labs, when each day that passes, someone else is being victimized and changed. I can't, not for me, not for Alex, or the friend who helped me escape and kept me sane afterward."

"Leann." His anguish was obvious in his voice, and I pressed closer for comfort—his and mine.

The warmth of his body against mine, the feel of his stubble on my palm, the smell of cinnamon, smoke, and that tantalizing musk that was uniquely his stirred longing within me. He was bad for my resolve, dangerous to my heart. And in that moment, I didn't care. My hand went around his neck and pressed, while the other circled his middle and pulled him closer. "I would love to stay here and be your mate," I breathed. "You bring light to my otherwise dreary existence; you make me yearn for more."

Ravi's throat bobbed, and I pressed on, needing him to understand, to absolve me of the guilt I was feeling inside. "If I leave things unresolved, I will never be able to fully relax, always wondering about the things I left undone. Alex—he was taken because of me. I need to find him, even if there's nothing but dust and bones to find."

Ravi exhaled, his breath fanning my face. The tension on his shoulders eased and his hands curved around my waist. "I understand," he said quietly. "I would come with you if I could."

"But you can't, and I can't stay." An idea struck me, impulsive and selfish, but it felt so right. I stroked the back of his neck. "This thing between us, I'd like to give it a try. I can't promise you forever, but I can give us sometimes. A month here, two weeks there. What do you say?"

He took so long to answer, I was afraid of what he'd say.

"If that's the only way I can be with you, then I'd like that."

I wanted to be happy about that, but what I felt was an ache so deep, it pierced my soul.

"It'll never be enough," Ravi murmured, touching his forehead to mine.

"I know." I kissed the corner of his mouth, then fitted my lips over his. "We're both here now." I nipped his bottom lip and the gesture broke through whatever restraint he had been holding to. I rejoiced. His mouth covered mine hungrily, possessively. I opened up and groaned when his tongue stroked mine.

Ravi bent, cupped my ass, his hands like two branding irons, even over the fabric of my pants. With a hop and his support, my legs wrapped around his lean waist. A tree trunk pushed against my back in the next second and our teeth clacked.

"You make me crazy," he whispered against my cheek. His mouth trailed down my neck and his hand dipped under my shirt, rough and searing. I reached for his belt, undid the hoop, and stuck my hand inside his pants. Ravi broke the kiss just as I found him, hot and ready. He hissed and grabbed my wrist. His forehead touched mine. His expression was pained, mouth twisted, eyes closed.

"If you don't want this to go any further," he panted, "I suggest we stop now."

In response, I swiped my thumb up and down. Whatever tenuous control he still possessed snapped. He shuddered, let go of my hand, speared his fingers into my hair and plunged his tongue into my mouth. Pleasure sparked between us, wild and desperate, burning away any residual reservation we had to dust.

We ended up on the ground. The world around us—the smell of damp earth and verdant foliage, the snap of branches and the creek of tall trees, the dark of the woods and the calls of night animals—all bearing witness to our moment of passion.

We came to our senses just as the last of the fireworks broke above the woods. I slumped against Ravi's heaving chest and panted against his neck. His arms went around me and squeezed.

"You okay?" he asked.

"I may need help walking, but otherwise, I've never been better."

"Next time, we'll go slowly. And on a bed."

A thrill went down my spine at the promise. I wanted that. I wanted him. I wanted him more than I did ten minutes ago. But there wasn't going to be a next time, not any time soon.

The more reason to bask in the here and now.

I dropped a kiss on his neck. "I'm good here. I don't need a bed."

Ravi groaned. "That's because you don't have rocks poking you in the ass."

"Such a baby."

I squealed when he pinched my ass and scrambled to my feet.

"Besides, we still have an appointment to keep."

And just like that, our moment was gone. Like a bucket of ice water, his words smothered my remaining lust into ash.

Chapter 23

The facility where the KKM experts conducted their tests was less than a hundred meters ahead, a squat building surrounded by trees on all sides. It looked like a cabin with a wraparound porch and large double doors. It had no windows that I could see, no guards, and no visible defenses.

"You're sure this is the right place?" I asked, mostly to air the doubt I was feeling. If the Kukona mineral was so valuable, why were the experts in an isolated house in the woods?

"It's an underground facility," Ravi explained as we climbed the two steps to the double doors. This close, I could tell they weren't made of wood—the impression I'd gotten from further away.

Ravi pressed a hidden button to the side of the doorframe and the doors parted with a hiss of air. I raised an eyebrow at him as if to say "see?". *So easy.*

He smiled secretively, placed a guiding hand on my lower back and led
 me in.

We came into a small foyer no larger than two meters by two meters, made more confined by the desk and the man seated behind it. He said something in Krozalian, and Ravi replied with a curt nod.

"What did he say?" I asked.

"Doctor Lamis is expecting us," he translated as we crossed to the second door, this one smooth and metallic gray.

There were no hinges or visible knobs, but it parted when we neared. The chamber we stepped in next was made of tinted glass—the floor, the walls, even the ceiling. It didn't reflect the light or our images, and it echoed with our steps and our breaths.

I had a feeling I was looking at one of the facility's defenses, but couldn't tell in which form it came as. Poisonous gas? Laser blasts? Flames, or ice?

We were met by two Kroz standing guard on the other side, a big space filled with surveillance equipment, and hunched tech personnel manning each. I counted five Kroz, each seated in front of two screens.

The two guards signaled and began escorting us away. No one we passed spared us a glance. Our escorts each keyed a password on the left and right side of the next door. There came twin bleeps, the keypads flashed red, and both Kroz pressed their thumbs and pinkie fingers to the scanner. Two more bleeps, another red flash, and then they scanned their retinas.

"Ooh, that looks hard to break," Mac said in my ear. "I wonder what would happen if one was slower than the other?"

The door opened with a hiss of air and the smell of synthetic materials. This time, we weren't greeted by another room, but a brightly lit staircase going down.

One of the escorts went first, followed by me, then Ravi, and a glance back showed our second escort had stopped at the landing.

After all the security above, I'd expected we'd be frisked or go through another checkpoint. Instead, we were taken to the first door on the left, into a capacious laboratory, filled with unfamiliar, quietly humming equipment, and a narrow examination bed.

The hairs on my body stood at attention, the feeling reminiscent of the one I'd had earlier when I'd come close to the KKM lift door. I scanned the shelves and the equipment, but there was no polished purple in the room. Nowhere that I could see anyway. My body, however, told me another story. Somewhere in this room was a lot of Kukona mineral.

The sole occupant of the room was a Kroz woman clad in whites and blues and holding a tablet. She glanced over when we entered, gray and yellow-slitted eyes moving from Ravi to me and back again.

"Lord Drax," she greeted curtly.

"Doctor Lamis."

"This is the human female I was told about?" She put down the tablet and came over, looking me up and down with a clinical assessment. "Please have a seat. What's your name?"

"Leann."

"All right, Leann," she began as she opened a drawer beside the narrow bed. "Have you been told why you are here?"

I gave Ravi a questioning look, unsure what to say. The doctor caught that and stopped. "Did you tell her why she's here?"

My impression of the woman went up a notch at the seriousness of her tone.

"We know she's here for a physical," Ravi said. "But explain what that will entail."

The woman's eyebrows went up and she glanced from Ravi to me. "Is this the captain I've been hearing about? The woman you're courting?" She waved her hand. "Sorry, it's none of my business. It's just there's a lot of gossip and speculation over the woman you've chosen as a life-mate."

Because she'd returned her focus to the drawer, she didn't see the way Ravi's eyes darkened, or how the amusement had drained from his expression. I tried to catch his attention, but he kept it firmly on the doctor's back.

"Vera asked to be notified when you arrived." She gave our escort a nod. "Please call the castle and let Vera Oshar know we're ready to commence."

The guard bowed and left.

"Should we wait until she arrives?" Doctor Lamis asked Ravi.

"No. There's no need to prolong this. I'll give the emperor my verbal report to go along with yours."

"Very well," the doctor said and turned to me. "I'll explain things as I go, and any time you wish to stop, you only need say so." Doctor Lamis pulled a large silver box out of the bottom drawer. "I'm going to examine the cybernetic capacity of your prosthetics first." She pulled on medical gloves. "I was told it contains traces of KKM?"

I nodded.

"Please, sit or lie down." She propped the box atop the table, opened the clasps, and revealed a familiar toolbox.

"Holy shit," Mac exclaimed. "Doesn't Baltsar use that same kit?"

My mouth dried at the needle-like tipped screwdriver Doctor Lamis selected.

"The right side, correct?" she asked and motioned to my arm. "I'm going to insert this needle into the median cubital. It'll cause some discomfort as it nullifies any Kukona-made parts and gives me a reading of all its uses."

My heart just about exploded in my chest as panic flooded my mouth with saliva. Ravi's hand closed around mine and squeezed.

"It'll be fine," he reassured me.

"It—this is a KKM examiner?" I asked, pointing at the toolbox and the familiar monitor inside it.

"Something like that. It'll determine its age, when it was mined and molded, how much amplification vibes it gives out, whether it's in balance or spiking, its radiation properties, and the condition of its symbiotic presence in your body. There are other technical readings as well, but those will depend on the primary results."

Doctor Lamis waited for me to ask something, but when I didn't, she inserted the needle into the vein in the crook of my elbow and released the e-spikes. Half my body immediately shut down. My right vision dimmed, not losing sight completely, but had this been permanent, I would have needed thick glasses to see.

Doctor Lamis looked into my eyes and exhaled. "Good, you're still here."

Ravi stiffened. "What does that mean?" he demanded.

The doctor gave him a sad smile. "I'm sorry. I detest politics. It's why I'm in here instead of the top offices in the KKM quarry."

"What does that mean?" Ravi repeated with a snarl.

Doctor Lamis paled. "I-I," she began and backed away until she hit the table beside the bed and flinched.

I grabbed Ravi's wrist with my left hand and squeezed. "Means zis was anozer zest," I lisped.

"Yes, yes," Doctor Lamis nodded emphatically, but Ravi wasn't looking at her. No, he was watching the way my entire right side had gone dead.

I lowered my eyes—or the left one, since the right no longer responded to brain signals. I was suddenly self-conscious, fearful to meet his eyes and find disgust or condemnation. I didn't think I'd take that well. Not now, not after what we'd shared.

"Test?" he growled. That one word came out like a threat. "What kind of test?"

Doctor Lamis' swallow was so loud, I heard it with my ordinary hearing. "That she's not a hypermorph."

I made an involuntary low noise in the back of my throat. *What had Baltsar been doing?*

Misreading my distress, Doctor Lamis hurried to explain, "To be fair, I knew you weren't one from the moment I laid eyes on you. Although the last hypermorph caught was before my time here, hypermorphs are programmed to self-destruct, to prevent anyone from tracking them back to their makers."

Was that what Baltsar was doing? Checking to see if Mac had taken over by disabling the KKM in my body? Because Mac hadn't been programmed to self-destroy at the sight of the silver box.

Something crashed against the far wall and shattered like glass. Doctor Lamis squeaked. I looked up. Ravi had his back turned, shoulders shaking, his fists clenched. Then he walked out. We listened for his footsteps. They stopped somewhere outside, but not so far that he couldn't be back in seconds if he wanted to.

"I'm sorry," Doctor Lamis murmured.

I waved my left hand at her. "S'okay." Had I known this would happen, I'd have asked Ravi to sit outside. Outburst aside, having him see me like this, only half human, made me feel exposed, more vulnerable than I'd ever been in my life.

Doctor Lamis pulled the monitor from the box and began fiddling with it. It looked exactly like the one Baltsar used, and it brought me no comfort, only questions. I had no doubt that Doctor Lamis was not trying to calibrate any of my mechanical parts, or even checking to make sure everything was working in order.

What else was this silver box hiding?

"I've never tested KKM on a living being before," Doctor Lamis said with a frown. "Please, let me know if it hurts or if there's any discomfort."

A door to my left slid open and a Kroz dressed in white moved in. He had a bundle underneath one arm, salt-and-pepper hair, and a tanned complexion. Our eyes met and…recognition surged through my body like a bolt of pure electricity.

The last time I'd looked into those eyes, the pupils had been round, not slitted. Which one was the lie? Human or Kroz?

"Doctor Reme," Doctor Lamis greeted. "Are you here for the inspection?"

Doctor Reme. The last time I'd seen him, I was lying prone on a bed, a person made of parts and pain, unable to function with any cohesion.

My thought flashed back ten years to a memory I'd forgotten but that was as clear as day now.

"Where do you want her, sir?" a bored voice asked from behind me.

Brown, human eyes examined my naked body without compassion. "She needs programming. Take her to the system engineer in Laboratory 9."

A shiver of remembrance zinged through my body, bringing goosebumps and dawning horror.

"Doctor Reme?" Doctor Lamis prompted.

Doctor Reme smiled, his eyes never leaving mine. "We meet again," he said, voice gravelly.

The thing about my mechanical side was that when shut down, it was nothing but a hundred-kilo pile of junk that kept me immobile. So, when Doctor Reme pointed his bundle at me—a bundle that looked like it ended in a narrow barrel—all I could do was push myself sideways with my left arm and leg. I almost wasn't strong enough. Hot pain pierced my side just as I managed to unbalance myself and fell off the bed. I hit my head on the hard ground, and although I didn't entirely feel the impact, I saw stars nonetheless. My vision went white and my brain felt like it was jostling loosely in my skull.

There was a thunk, a crash—or six—in the time it took my brain to stop vibrating. The ringing in my ears continued though, and above all else was Ravi's snarls.

I tried to get to my feet, to move, but all I managed was to slide and flop onto my back.

A flat, gray object flew over my head and crashed against something to my right. The fumes of pungent and acidic chemicals invaded my senses and made my left eye water. I reached for the needle in my arm. I needed to get up, and I needed to be able to move for that.

Cool, rubber-coated fingers stopped me. "Wait," Doctor Lamis said urgently. "If you pull it out without disconnecting, your cybernetics could glitch."

I debated ignoring her, but something told me to wait. She crawled back to the silver box just as footsteps ran out the door, followed by another. I listened until both sets faded out of my hearing range.

"There," the doctor said and pulled the needle from my elbow. My right side sparked back to life and I pushed myself into a sitting position.

The once-pristine lab was in shambles, broken glass, overturned equipment and furniture, and blood.

"Whoa!" Mac shouted. "What the tinkling balls is going

on? What the hell happened?"

"There was a Kroz doctor," I said. "He had round pupils the last time I saw him ten years ago."

Mac hissed. "From the dark lab? Son of a bitch! I knew the Kroz was involved."

I scrambled to my feet, my right side feeling clumsy and heavy, still not yet at full capacity.

"I want to hear more about that," I told Mac.

The cabinet behind me had a large hole in the middle, the edges smoking faintly. Doctor Reme had meant to kill me. Not capture, not examine, but kill. The silver toolbox was on the ground, its contents strewn all over. Along other tools I couldn't identify was the bundle Doctor Reme held, the laser gun that had been concealed inside now fully visible. And there was blood everywhere. On the bed, myself, the floor.

"You're bleeding," Doctor Lamis stated, reaching for my left arm.

I yanked it away and the world tilted. Something wet ran down my cheek. A finger swipe told me I had a cut on my right temple. A headache was blooming there too, and as if given permission by the acknowledgment, my left arm started throbbing.

"Let me see," Doctor Lamis tried again.

"No," I said and took a step away, glad the world remained steady. "I have to go." I ran out the door, only to stumble over a body. I'd have face-planted on the floor if it wasn't for Ravi.

He circled my waist and pulled me upright as if I weighed nothing. Doctor Reme's body lay on the floor, neck crooked and his eyes, brown and with round pupils, vacant. His nose was busted and still leaked blood, along with the split lip. They hadn't had the chance to swell, and never would.

I grabbed Ravi and searched for any injuries. Save for the wrath burning in his yellow eyes, he looked fine. "You okay?" I asked while patting him down and leaving bloody stains as I went.

He grabbed my hand and pressed it against his chest, his other raising my chin so he could examine the gash on my temple. His heart was beating so fast: boom, boom, boom, boom, boom, boom.

"You okay?" I asked again. "Were you hit?"

Doctor Lamis appeared at the door, her complexion bloodless.

"Who's he?" Ravi demanded.

I looked down at Doctor Reme. "His name is Geovanni Reme," I said. "He was a prosthetic technician—I had forgotten about him until today. I thought he was human then."

"Halfling," Ravi replied. "You call them hybrid humans."

I knew that now. I'd never met a hybrid human who could shift their eyes at will, but I'd heard rumors about it. Absently, I wondered if Baltsar could do the same.

Doctor Lamis gasped, bringing Ravi's wrath in her direction. He took a step her way, but I didn't move from his path.

"Who's he?" he demanded again, making sure to aim the question at the doctor.

"S-she's right. His name is-was Doctor Geovanni Reme. I don't know why—where—I don't understand." She looked at me, then down at the body, and shook her head. "I don't understand. He was Kroz."

"He's a Halfling, more human than Kroz. You can tell that from the way the pupils reverted to human after death. If you run an autopsy, you'll find characteristics of both races. How long has he worked here?"

"He's our field expert. He's been here since before I joined twelve years ago."

"The other one?" Ravi asked.

There was another one?

"Dar Yun. Doctor Reme's assistant."

Ravi looked down at me.

I shook my head. I didn't recognize the name.

"Who's their supervisor?"

Imperial Stardust

Before Lamis could answer, an explosion rocked the building, sending us tumbling like chess pieces. Then came a piercing roar, followed by the most haunting wail I'd ever heard.

Chapter 24

The world trembled around us. For an eternal moment, I couldn't tell if it was the blasting cry that made my brain quake or if the ground under my body was shaking. Something crashed inside the lab, but glasses could break from high-pitched noises too, so that still didn't answer the question.

The wailing sound went on, getting impossibly louder, piercing my eardrums and brain like stabbing knives. My thoughts skittered back and forth, bouncing like pinballs, not processing anything. Mac was saying something over and over, but even that was hard to understand.

Except for the agonizing pain. That, I could feel and fully comprehend.

I covered my ears with both hands to no avail, my body trembling as if it wanted to break apart. The ground bucked and hurled me against the wall, and I knew then for certain that the ground was actually shaking.

Earthquake.

On the heels of that realization came the thought that we were in the basement and that at any moment, the structure could fall and bury us alive. I thought that was what Mac was telling me as well, to get up and find a safe spot to wait for the tremors to subside. Only, I couldn't move.

There was a pop inside my head, and warm blood began tracking down my palm and wrist. A glance at Ravi, down on all fours, told me his nose and ears were bleeding too. I didn't have the strength to check on Doctor Lamis, much less get up those stairs. Neither could Ravi, from what I'd seen. I rolled against the wall and let myself lie there, blood-soaked hands covering my ears, and hoped this torture would end soon.

I wasn't sure when the deafening wails stopped because the ringing inside my head continued for a few more minutes, but I did notice when it began to abate. I could hear Ravi speaking, and I could hear Doctor Lamis sobbing. The ground, however, continued shaking.

"This is the Tanue," Ravi whispered, or maybe he shouted and I just couldn't hear clearly. But it was the stricken grief in his eyes that had me strumming with dread.

"I don't understand," I whispered back.

"The emperor," he said. "The emperor is dead. I wasn't alive when this happened last, but this is the Tanue. It's grieving the loss."

Ravi, Doctor Lamis, and I were the sole survivors in the facility. We passed three more people with their necks twisted, but the rest had been killed by a laser blast, presumably by Doctor Reme—or his assistant. All the monitoring equipment on the main floor had been destroyed, some by the earthquake, most by a laser blast.

I didn't know what that meant. What I did know was that not everyone in the facility had been killed by the same person. I assumed that any destruction caused by a laser blast was done by Doctor Reme, and the others by Ravi.

The more I uncovered, the deeper I realized this KKM conspiracy went. There wasn't merely one individual in the Krozalian upper echelons smuggling KKM, but an entire group. Whether this group and the rebellion were connected was the question circling my mind. Had Doctor Reme's timing and the emperor's death been a coincidence?

My brain was too addled for me to ponder the ramifications of this scenario. I also had no time to stop and think it over.

How and why Ravi was certain of the emperor's fate remained elusive to me. But I assumed that it had to do with the lingering aftershocks and that horrible wail.

We reached the clearing in front of the facility on a run. I was able to keep up with Ravi's longer strides, but Doctor Lamis was soon left in our wake. Or maybe she chose to stay back.

We hit the road for the castle a moment later. Instead of taking the left and sprinting up the path, Ravi continued in a straight line, across the road, and into the underbrush.

"Where are you going?" I called.

"The emperor had a meeting in the imperial garden. I left him there with Vera and the rest. He...if he's dead, I need to find the princess."

I swore. "She was with him?"

"No, she shouldn't be. She was with Zafra."

"I can see the garden. There are people there, but I don't see the emperor or bodies," Mac said. "I can't spot the princess either, but most of the garden is obscured by trees and a gazebo."

"Keep looking," I ordered.

We ran in silence after that. I was able to keep up with Ravi, but his stamina surpassed mine. By the time we reached the top of the bluff where the castle sat, I was sticky with sweat and breathing hard, dying for a break. But he kept going, and I pressed on.

The imperial garden was exactly that: a garden fit for an emperor, filled with tall sculptures made of glass and gleaming metal. They nestled among squat trees, tall trees, and flowers of all shapes, colors, and sizes, framed in the back by the side of the towering castle. We slowed when a sprawling gazebo came into view, and Ravi motioned for me to wait. I wanted to follow him as he flitted from shadow to shadow, but I was breathing too fast, my panting too loud for any modicum of stealth. If there were enemies there, they'd hear me coming from a distance.

"I can see three individuals across from you," Mac told me. "About fifty meters into the trees."

"Armed?"

"Can't see weapons, but they could be primed to use magic."

"Are they heading this way?"

"No. Toward a lagoon."

"Anyone else?" I asked, scanning my surroundings and seeing no one.

"Not in the open."

Which meant there could be others closing in on Ravi. I concentrated on my breathing and tried slowing it down. It took me about two infinite minutes. With Mac's guidance, I followed the path Ravi had taken into the gazebo. I found him kneeling by a prone body, applying pressure to a wound I couldn't see. Except for the ominous dark pool under the person and the way red contrasted with the pale skin of her breasts.

"Press here," Ravi said to me. "I need to see if there's anyone else."

I dropped to my knees on the other side of the body.

Vera.

Blood bubbled out of her mouth and trickled down her cheeks. She was dying, and we all knew it. I put pressure on the fist-sized wound on her chest anyway. Her eyes were closed, her lungs whistling like a blown balloon.

"Vera?" I said softly.

Her eyes fluttered but didn't open.

"Who did this?" I asked. "Come on, Vera, help me here."

Her eyes opened. They were glazed and unfocused. I brought my face closer, blocking her field of vision. "Who did this?" I repeated.

Vera's hand twitched. Her index finger stiffened. I followed to where it pointed at the back of the gazebo. But all I could see were limbs, blood, and gore. Maybe she wasn't pointing her finger in answer to my question. Unless she'd killed whoever had done this and the body lay somewhere in that direction. Or maybe her perception was skewed.

Ravi was crouched over another body a few meters away. I recognized the platinum wedding band on the figure's pinky: Emperor Rokoskiv's. I looked away and back to where Vera's finger had pointed.

"What's in there?" I asked her, but her finger had curled and her eyes had closed. "Engage infrared," I said sub-vocally, and the right side of my vision switched to patches of red and cool blues.

"Damn, damn, and double damn," Mac chanted. "Scan the rest."

I turned my head and found three more patches.

"They're covered from above by those Baleq trees," Mac said. "Be careful."

I did a three-sixty sweep, but aside from those five, I couldn't find more body heat.

I clicked my thumb and forefinger, and Ravi's head raised. His eyes were two shadowed pools. My heart ached for his loss.

I pointed to where two Kroz were crouched and raised two fingers. He cocked his head. I mimed holding a weapon and shooting. I turned to the spot where the other three had been, but they had vanished.

Fuck. It took me a few nerve-wracking moments to find them again, and that only because they were moving. Heading to the front. If we didn't leave now, they'd hem us in.

Vera's finger brushed against my ankle. I glanced down and found her trying to speak, coughing blood instead. I shook my head. I didn't understand.

"The princess," she mouthed carefully. "Royal wing."

"We'll get her," I promised. "We'll keep her safe."

Vera inhaled a burbling breath, then exhaled one last time. Her eyes went unseeing and I shut them gently, leaving blood smears on her lids and upper cheeks. "We'll keep her safe," I vowed again.

Ravi was barricading the entrance with an upturned bench. There was the sound of a laser discharging, followed by a few more. Ravi pulled his laser gun from an ankle holster and shot blindly from left to right, then right to left.

I engaged the infrared vision again and scanned outside. The foliage didn't allow me to see far, but from the distance between the red spots among the greens, there were more people out there than the night revealed. At least six. But they weren't coming any closer, even with all the sculptures and tree trunks they could use as cover.

"Why aren't they pressing their advance?"

"Maybe they're not planning to engage," Mac guessed. "I think Kroz magic needs line of sight to work."

They hadn't engaged Vera with magic.

Ravi fired a few laser blasts, and the Kroz outside responded. Their shots were wild, some of them not even reaching the gazebo.

"Maybe they need to keep the two of you inside so they have time to deal with something else."

Or someone. Like the princess.

I picked up a bloodied, sticky laser from the ground and moved to where Ravi took cover.

"It's a diversion," I told him. "I think they're going for the princess."

Ravi's jaw flexed. "I can't see them. I need visuals to get a lock on them."

I peeked over the bench. Ravi swore. I dodged his reaching arm and moved around him. I peeked again. "There are six." I pointed to where I saw the red blobs. "The two that were hiding in the back seemed to have joined the others in the front."

"The lagoon, the princess was heading for the lagoon. It's about a hundred meters in that direction."

"They want you to think that they're there to block your path to the lagoon," Mac concluded at the same time I recognized the ploy.

"They want us to try to get through them," I said.

"There are others by the lagoon," Mac said. "Three that I can see, but it's heavily treed as well."

"Dolenta is not there," I told Ravi. "She's in the royal wing. Vera told me."

Ravi didn't ask me if I was sure. He picked up his commlink and told someone to abort the lagoon and head for the castle.

Somewhere outside, an explosion went off. Screams and

the sound of a laser fight reached us a second later.

"We could try getting through the back and leave from there," I suggested.

Ravi snarled when a lucky blast hit the edge of the bench and sent chipped rock everywhere. "It's a cliff wall."

"That side?" I pointed to our right.

"Clear view from the castle. There are two laser snipers."

Before I could ask, he said, "It's how Vera and the others got shot."

Ravi's commlink beeped and he glanced down at it. "There's a barricade at the castle entrance." He tapped a key. "Furox and Rodil, take the kitchens. Zafra, whoever's with you, take the terrace. Anyone near the main road, pick someone and see if you can get in through the caves. Whoever gets in first, notify us so we can follow, but don't wait. Head to the royal wing. I'll meet you there."

Ravi spared me a brief glance.

"Incoming!" Mac shouted in my ear. "Plas grenade."

"Fuck." I pushed Ravi down and covered as much of his body as I could, arms protecting his head. The sound of the grenade hitting the ground and rolling away was faint. But I saw the moment Ravi realized what it was and what I was doing. He began shifting, but the blast came in the next moment and everything went black.

Chapter 25

I didn't stay down for long. That was the beauty of having half my body made of unbendable metal. Not counting the indestructible Kukona mineral that gave fast healing and endurance.

Ravi was leaning over me, eyes completely yellow with not a brown or orange speck, his mouth pursed with strain. The smell of blood and hot iron was thick in the air, along with dust and upturned earth.

"Are you taking advantage of my unconscious body?" I croaked.

Ravi flinched. His head raised, face drawn with grief and devastation. His throat bobbed when he swallowed. He looked like a man who'd watched his entire world be destroyed while he sat safely watching atop a hill.

I did that. I put that look in his eyes.

"Hey. I'm okay," I said softly, touching his face. It came out sticky with blood. "I'm fine."

"Don't ever do that again," he rasped. "Never put your life at risk for mine."

"I knew I'd survive." Though I really didn't. I'd never tried blowing up myself to see if I'd come out the other side.

He didn't look convinced, so I sat up, suppressing the groan of pain the motion caused. I took in the devastation in the gazebo, or what had once been the gazebo. Now, it looked like a giant animal had raged in the space, digging up flowers and dirt and breaking the walls.

"You're hurt," I said, taking in the blood-soaked sleeve of his tunic.

Ravi huffed a humorless laugh. "I'm hurt? I'm hurt? I got a scratch compared to—"

I touched my mouth to his, shutting him up. "I'm well," I said, leaning a hair's breadth away. "And my injuries will be healed by tomorrow." I waited until the yellow shifted to orange, then brushed my mouth against his again.

He helped me stand, one arm circling my waist. "Come on, we need to go."

I heard it then, the sound of muffled footsteps coming our way.

"There's a small alcove by the cliff. We'll make our stand there." He helped me limp through the dust and debris, both of us bent over to present smaller targets. But no one shot at us, and a glance back told me why: a sculpture had fallen across where the entrance should have been, blocking most of it. But they could still climb over it, and we were running out of time.

Ravi wasn't joking. The lip of the cliff was less than fifteen meters away. We ran for it, though my leg kept cramping. My back burned with my movements, and I could feel blood trickling down my shoulder and pooling on the waistband of my pants. I was more injured than I'd guessed.

Ravi directed me to the right, toward a large boulder. We were almost upon it when I saw the narrow pass leading down. Well, it wasn't a pass, just a narrow ridge that looked to have been formed naturally.

"This ends in an alcove that can't be seen from above," Ravi said. "Can you make it?"

There was only one right answer. I considered telling Ravi to go first and discarded the thought in the next breath. There was no reason why I should start an argument when we didn't have the time to spare. Either the ridge would hold my weight and I'd make it to the alcove, or it wouldn't. Either way, if we stayed here, we'd both die. I took a long breath and stepped onto the ridge. It barely covered my toes. I found small divots for my fingertips and began making my way. The cliffside curved about a meter off, and I spotted the alcove Ravi mentioned. It was less than five meters down from the edge of the cliff above, and less than that from me.

Somewhere above, a man shouted something. I gritted my teeth and forced myself not to hurry, carefully choosing handholds and testing them out. To my left, I could hear Ravi following, the whisper of his shoes on the ridge, the rustling of his clothes against the rock face. And then I reached the alcove and stepped in. I hadn't realized how much my arms shook until I lowered them to my sides.

Ravi stepped in behind me, pulling me deeper—against the smooth stone of the alcove. He held me for a few seconds, breathing me in, hands rubbing against my sides and aggravating some of my injuries. I bit my lip and let him hold me, aware he needed the reassurance. I patted him on the back.

"We should check on the others," I finally said.

He grunted, stepped back, and checked his commlink.

"Anything?" I murmured.

"No."

"Do you think they'll follow us here?"

"No. If they know about this alcove, they'll know I have the advantage."

We both looked out, our vantage showing us the twinkling stars in the clear sky and the churning, dark waters of the sea. We were safe for now, but we couldn't stay here and wait for the world to right itself.

"Where will Dolenta be in the royal wing?" I asked, the beginnings of a crazy plan forming in my head.

"Her room, probably. It's the highest tower on the south side, facing the cliffs." Ravi shook his head. "There's no way to climb that tower. Any imperfections have been sanded smooth centuries ago. Our only option is to wait for the attackers to leave."

"They're not going to," Mac interjected.

I didn't think they would.

"Satellite view shows two sentries: one by the boulder and another by the destroyed gazebo. Both have a clear view of the cliff."

I sat cross-legged in the corner and leaned my uninjured shoulder against the rock. "Do you have visual inside the castle yet?" I asked sub-vocally.

"Almost. But I think I should point out that if I'd been allowed to do this before, we'd already have eyes on the princess."

I closed my eyes and began loosening my mental shield. "Forget about it. We'll extract her with the *Splendor*. The highest tower facing the cliff shouldn't be difficult to find."

"Are you sure?" Mac asked. "If you do this, there's no plausible deniability to lean back on."

"We don't have any other options."

"Sure you do. I know this is cold and heartless, but this is not your battle to fight."

"Mmm."

I let my mental shield drop and connected my mind to Mac's, then pushed further with Mac's help. It took more than I'd anticipated to synchronize with the *Splendor*, and even more to power up the engines. By then, Mac and I were one with the ship, our connection wide open the way I'd only dared do once, not so long ago. We only had one chance to get this right and a handful of minutes for that chance to succeed.

The spaceport was quiet around us, though still brightly lit. There were several ships in the hangars, more than there had been when I'd docked, but they all had their engines off. Both the doors and roof were sealed for the night, so I primed our laser, ready to blast the way out. The moment the *Splendor's* weapons came online, an alarm blared inside the port, and statistics began scrolling in my mind.

I lifted a few meters off the ground, rotated, and blasted the doors off.

Everything was fully charged, and I put the shields on standby, ready for activation. I flew towards the castle, ascending to the highest tower facing south. It took about three minutes to get there. The doors to the balcony were open, and I angled to see inside the room.

There were five people inside, barricaded behind overturned furniture as they fired at a large hole in the far wall. I lowered closer to the balcony, careful to align the cargo ramp with the railing. A shot hit the hull, powerful enough to scratch but not to cause damage.

Zafra was facing the balcony, still dressed in her floral dress, holding a laser gun aimed at the ship. To her other side crouched Lorenzo, Cassandra, and another Kroz with white-cropped hair. They kept whoever was on the other side of the hole in the wall occupied under a barrage of laser fire. Dolenta was crouched beside Cassandra, holding a laser gun and looking dazed but otherwise unharmed.

I let the cargo ramp open a fraction and spoke through the intercom. My voice was a bit mechanical but still recognizable. "It's me. Time to go."

Zafra didn't wait. I liked her efficiency. She dropped beside Lorenzo and said something. He tapped Cassandra's shoulder and pointed at the *Splendor*. In turn, Cassandra crawled to the princess and spoke in her ear. The next moment, Zafra and the other Kroz stood and sent a barrage of laser blasts at the hole, giving cover for Cassandra to help Dolenta to stand and dash for the *Splendor*, Lorenzo covering them from behind.

Two ships appeared on my starboard side, still far enough that they were only pinpricks, but close enough that they'd be here in seconds.

Statistics told me if we didn't leave within the next twenty seconds, we would have to engage those ships. I didn't want to be there in twenty seconds. "Zafra. Come on," I urged.

Cassandra and Dolenta jumped, Followed by Lorenzo. They hit the cargo ramp and scrambled inside. "We have to go now." To Dolenta, I said, "Strap in, princess. This is going to get rough."

The white-haired Kroz picked up the barrage while Zafra ran for the ship. She jumped over the railing and was airborne the next second, hitting the ramp still running. Back in the room, the white-haired Kroz jerked and fell, throat blown apart by a laser blast.

More Kroz came pouring through the hole in the wall and into Dolenta's room than I'd expected. They were all wearing full armor. Two carried between them a portable plas cannon.

While Zafra's laser blasts did nothing but scratch the hull, portable plas cannons could cause significant damage. Like a hole on the bulkhead. The only reason I suspected they hadn't blown everyone to bits was because it needed time to charge, and they'd already used it once to create that hole in the wall. They probably hadn't expected much resistance from the princess.

Whatever their reason, the plas cannon was now primed, and it was aimed at the cargo bay, where the ramp had just shut. I dove sideways and rolled to keep the shot from grazing my port side, then another roll to even out. I didn't have the time to make sure everyone was all right, trusting that they understood this wasn't going to be a smooth flight. I headed next for my body and Ravi. I could vaguely feel him shaking me, trying to wake me up. Ships were coming my way and I didn't know if they were friend or foe.

I shot the boulder where Mac had told me a Kroz was waiting, then sent a few warning shots at the gazebo.

When I lowered in front of the tiny cave, Ravi was framed by the alcove, blocking the view of my body behind him. He had the laser gun aimed, but he didn't shoot. I lowered the ramp and maneuvered below the alcove so he could jump into the cargo bay.

Whether it was the sight of Dolenta and his sister inside or something else, he holstered his weapon, scooped up my body, and leaped.

I flew in a straight line for a few seconds, igniting both primary and secondary shields and giving Ravi sufficient time to strap in my body. Then I sped up and away from the two ships closing in.

I should have erected my mental shields then and piloted the ship manually, but I hadn't factored in the need to engage in

Imperial Stardust

combat when I'd concocted my plan. My foresight hadn't extended beyond rescuing the princess from the tower, maybe finding an isolated place to land and regroup.

"Strap in," I ordered over the intercom. "We might need to leave the atmosphere."

I sent two warning shots toward the ships closing in, purposefully missing and scattering them apart. I had no idea if they were friend or foe. But I wasn't going to take any chances. The incoming communication light blinked on. I could trace it back to the spaceport tower, but the dilemma of friend or foe held for the spaceport the same way it did for the approaching ships.

I analyzed our chances for evading the two ships without the need to leave Krozalia and the pros and cons of heading to space and hopping to Dupilaz Moon. Our chances of success in either option were nearly identical, with neither exceeding forty percent.

It was the hot sensation of the target lock to the *Splendor's* portside that decided for us. That, and the other three ships that bleeped into existence behind us. With a burst of speed that broke the sound barrier, we headed for space. I could feel my energy draining, and if I didn't want to be laid flat for the next few hours, I'd need to disconnect. But five ships were coming, and I couldn't see a way of losing them. Not without hopping. I wouldn't be able to go far, but far enough that I'd be able to shake them off.

"Ten seconds until zero gravity," I announced and maxed the speed the *Splendor* could endure in atmosphere. It wasn't much, but it was better than letting the pursuing ships close the gap any further.

Almost at the ten-second mark, Ravi dropped into the pilot's seat and began strapping in.

Three, two, one.

We punched into space like a well-timed fist. I pushed on the speed for a few seconds, aware that the five ships still had their target locks on and were primed to fire. I prepared to hop even as I arranged to change the *Splendor's* registration number. It wouldn't hold against scrutiny, but it would buy us additional time to plan our next move. Then I assigned Ravi control of the ship a second before we hopped.

My body had already spent energy healing my injuries, so I could only hold the hop for a brief moment before my consciousness began to give way. I had enough to push us out of the hop and make sure we didn't come out in another asteroid field.

We hadn't.

There was nothing around us but space and vacuum, and the radar confirmed the assessment.

We made it. The princess was safe.

At least for now. With that comforting thought, I let my consciousness float away.

Imperial Stardust

Epilogue

Lord Drax
Leann went limp in the co-pilot's seat, and I let out a symphony of profanities in several languages, along with concocted ones. We had emerged from the hop a few hours away from Dupilaz Moon, and a scan told me we had lost the pursuing ships.

"If you die," I snarled as my fingers danced on the console, "I'll ..." My words failed me. "Don't leave me." I finished making sure the ship was on course for Dupilaz Moon before I unclasped my harness and jumped out of my seat. My fingers were shaking as I checked Leann's pulse.

There, like a fast drum, but strong. I swallowed down the bile trying to escape my throat and brushed the loose hair away from her pale face. There was so much blood. How hadn't I seen how hurt she was?

There was much I hadn't seen, I thought. She had piloted the *Splendor* remotely, outmaneuvered the other ships, and managed to hop us to safety, all without needing to touch the controls. I understood what it meant. It nagged at me, yet, my main concern was her well-being.

"Leann?" I unfastened her harness and lifted her from her seat. I wasn't yet ready to take her from the bridge, so I laid her down on the floor and stripped off her tunic. It was soaked with blood and grit from the imperial garden. I grabbed a bottle of water from the side of her pilot's seat, took off my shirt, and soaked it through. As cleaning went, it wasn't the most sanitary method, but instinct told me fussing wasn't as necessary as making sure the wounds were cleaned from the grime.

I wiped her side where the damage from the plas bomb

was more severe, gritting my teeth as I remembered how she had protected me.

"You foolish woman," I murmured.

Her wounds were deep and raw, but no longer bleeding. I suspected that in a few hours, they would be nothing but scabs. "I don't know if I should shake you senseless or kiss you."

Both. I'll do both…when she wakes up.

The gash near her hip started bleeding again when I passed the wet shirt over it, wiping the soil that had lodged to the wound. I pressed the other side of the shirt to the wound, suddenly glad she wasn't awake for this.

"Maybe I should put you in the med unit."

"Some rest will suffice," a mechanical voice said from the console.

I whipped around, thinking for a moment that Leann was somehow communicating through her ship.

"Leann?"

"The name is Mac. As you can see for yourself, Leann is indisposed."

"Mac," I repeated. It was the name Leann had called after Thern had shot her. The name she had refused to explain. "You're—"

"The hypermorph the scientists intended to take over her body and mind."

I stiffened. "She's not a hypermorph."

"She isn't, no. But I am."

My brow creased. "The *Splendor*?"

"Wouldn't that make things easier? I can access the *Splendor* when necessary, although my main matrix is implanted in her wrist. Leann and I have gone through a lot together. But she's her own person, the same way I'm my own."

"So you're possessing the ship?"

Mac snorted. "If that makes you feel any better, sure."

I had a lot of questions, but my priority hadn't changed. "How do I wake her?" I asked, looking down at her prone body. My heart constricted at how lifeless she looked.

"She'll wake when she's ready. Let her rest. The more she does, the faster she'll heal."

"The med unit—"

"Isn't needed. Her body is already fighting the shock of mending so fast. If you push her to heal faster, you could put her in a coma."

I clenched my jaw. "How do I know you're not lying? You could be saying that to delay getting her the help she needs so when she dies, you could possess her fully."

The console let out a sigh that sounded a lot like a person put upon. "Take a closer look at her wounds."

I did. They looked raw still, but dry, the visible muscles turning a dull brown.

"In about two hours, they should be nothing but old wounds. In three, there will be nothing there but lingering soreness and bruises."

"Can-can you feel her pain?"

"No. I don't have control of her body or mind. If she's unconscious, I can't even communicate with her."

"So you watch over her. What would you do if there was a threat?"

"The same I'd do to you if you attempt anything funny."

"You threatening me?" The idea was so bizarrely surreal, I had the impulse to laugh.

"You'd be surprised. For one, I can turn off life support and watch you suffocate. Since you're sitting beside Leann, I won't risk harming her. But I can do it to your princess or sister, and I can definitely start spacing all of you. When Leann wakes, I'll tell her you decided to go and convince her to leave."

My mirth had died halfway through his threat. I stood. My hands clenched as I eyed the console, realizing that if the ship turned on us, there was nothing I could do to stop it.

"I'm not going to do that," Mac continued. "Because Leann is very fond of all of you, and I'd rather see her happy than sad. She's had enough sorrow in her life, and I suspect, if you're as open-minded as you seem to be, you can bring her the joy she deserves."

"But you wouldn't hesitate to kill everyone aboard if I threatened her," I concluded.

"I'm glad we understand each other. Now, please, take her to her bunk and let her rest."

I bent and picked her up, carefully cradling her so not to aggravate her wounds. At the door to the bridge, I paused, though I suspected there wasn't a place on the ship that Mac couldn't hear me. "I'd give up my life to keep her safe, and if she lets me, I'll strive to bring her joy for as long as I breathe."

"I know," Mac replied quietly.

I strolled out of the bridge with Leann in my arms, feeling like I had just passed the most important test of my life.

***

Leann's journey will continue in *Book 3, Eclipsed Crown*, the final installment in The MacLee Chronicles.

Order your copy here.

Subscribe to my newsletter to be the first to know about new releases, read excerpts, and receive updates on my writing.

I love to chat with readers, so if you'd like to say hi, ask questions, engage with other readers, or be the first to know about new releases and sales, come join my group https://www.facebook.com/groups/5454200234675036

Character and Glossary List (in alphabetic order)

Admiral Fulk: (human) high-ranking official for the CTF.

Alex Rubin: (human) co-pilot for the CTF.

Ashak: gland responsible for the storing and the channeling of Kroz magic, located near the vocal chords.

Atek Avenue: famous shopping strip on Krozalia.

Baleq Tree: towering trees native to Krozalia that releases relaxing and fragrant smells.

Bloyer Muz: (Cradox) Control Tower Supervisor on Station V-5.

Brofil: alien race native to Sector 7. They live on a blood-based diet and look human, save for a blue tinge to their skin.

Carindum: a smaller heart the Kroz is born with that stays inactive until the day they form a life-mate bond.

Captain Elias: (human) captain of the stealth ship Eagle 13.

Captain Jacobs: (race unspecified) captain of the Black Court—located on Cyrus Station.

Captain Sullivan, AKA Sunny: (human) captain for the Confederacy Task Force.

Cassandra, AKA Cassie: (human) system's engineer for the CTF.

Centaur's Gateway: closest gateway to Cyrus Station—goes from Sector 8 to Sector 7 and vice versa.

Cheche: small furry rodents native to Cyrus Station.

Colonists: humans who live in human colonies.

Commodore Lorenzo: (human) commodore for the CTF.

Comula: Krozalian dish made from sap from the Forlo tree, cooked with spices and flour.
Cordolis: capital of Krozalia.
Cradox: alien race native to Sector 9. Some are humanoid in shape, others are insectile. They've been warring with humans from Sector 8 for decades.
CTF: (human military) Confederacy Task Force.
Cyrus Station: station at the mid-point between two major gateways. Ruled by the Obsidian Court.
Dalman: (Kroz) royal warrior.
Dante's Gateway: gateway at the edge of Sector 8, close to Sector 9.
Dar Yun: (hybrid human) Doctor Geovanni Reme's assistant.
Derk: (Kroz) Furox and Rose's newborn son.
Doctor Geovanni Reme: (hybrid human) prosthetic technician.
Doctor Lamis: (Kroz) KKM expert.
Donnel: (Kroz) high-ranking official in the Krozalian government.
Dradja: person oath-sworn to protect someone at the cost of their own life.
Endoy: underwater city in Krozalia.
Esme: (Feromantics) seamstress.
Evo: (Kroz) royal warrior.
Felicia, AKA Dolenta Tsakid: (Kroz) Krozalian princess and future empress.
Firaz: (Kroz) royal warrior.
Flenna: (Kroz) castle guard and assassin.
Furox: (Kroz) Ravi's cousin and royal warrior.
HSA: Human Supreme Assembly—the human representative body for all the major space stations and colonies. Located on Earth and comprised of seven members, one from each Earth continent.
Jazzy: (Kroz) royal warrior.
Kebet Box: small device used to detect hypermorphs.

Koshka: Krozalian term of endearment.

Leann Smith, AKA Clara Colderaro: (human) once a captain for the CTF and now captain of her ship, the *Splendor*.

Leo: (race unspecified) hacker, Leann's informant.

Linsky: (Kroz) emperor's advisor and one of the rebellion leaders.

Lorvel: (Kroz) Ravi and Zafra's mother.

Mac: sentient AI embedded in Leann's wrist.

Mada: Kroz word for mother.

Meat-peckers: carrion birds native to Krozalia.

Milva: (Kroz) Furox's mother.

Moresy Cotelum: ancient and violent competition put in place to determine the next Krozalian ruler in the event the royal family has no heir left.

Obsidian Court: ruling body of Cyrus Station.

Ozvie: (Kroz) Ravi and Zafra's father.

Ravi Drax, AKA Madrovi Fidraxi: (Kroz) Krozalia's head guard, the emperor's left hand, and the Grim Reaper of the Galaxy.

Renzo: (Kroz) castle guard.

Rodil: (Kroz) royal warrior.

Rodona Gateway: gateway on Sector 5—Krozalian System.

Rokoskiv Tsakid: (Kroz) emperor of Krozalia, Dolenta's father, purportedly the most powerful person in the galaxy.

Salba: small uninhabitable planet near V-5 Station.

Sarkar: second largest city in Krozalia.

Shivarhi Blade: blade that can cut through steel.

Syam: (Kroz) royal warrior.

Tafari Ocean: located on the south of Krozalia.

Thern Boloski: (Kroz) Ravi's second in command.

Trawx: (Kroz) Linsky's guard.

Tregoe: (Kroz) royal warrior.

V-5 Station: artificial space station between Sector 8 and 9.

Vera Oshar: (Kroz) Emperor Rokaskiv's right hand,

spy, assassin, and Leann's lady's maid.
Voner: space pirates.
Vroj: uncle in Krozalian.
Vroja: aunt in Krozalian.
Wedva-Xa: translated to Dark Sky. Ravi's personal ship, destroyed near V-5 in an ambush.
Zafra: (Kroz) Ravi's sister and royal warrior.
Zefron: (Kroz) emperor's advisor and one of the rebellion leaders.

Imperial Stardust

Other books by Jina S. Bazzar

The MacLee Chronicles
Splendor's Orbit 1
Imperial Stardust 2
Eclipsed Crown 3

Shadow Walker Series
Shadow Walker 1
Shadow Pawn 2
Shadow Flames 3
Shadow War 4

The Roxanne Fosch Files
Heir of Ashes 1
Heir of Doom 2
Heir of Fury 3
The Curse (A Roxanne Fosch Files Novella)

The Archives of Innah McLeod
Crimson Spellscape 1
The Grosh Alliance 2 (coming summer 2024)

From Fame to Ruin: A Gripping Standalone Romantic Suspense Novel

About the author

Jina Bazzar is a Palestinian author, born and raised in Brazil. Like most writers, her love of books began at a young age. Unlike most writers, she never aspired to become one.
It was only years after she became blind that she tried her hand at writing, giving voice to all the wild, rambling thoughts in her mind.
She now lives in Palestine with her family, taking inspiration from the smallest things in life. When she's not writing or networking on social media, you can find her in the kitchen, baking while listening to (often very loud) music.

Printed in Great Britain
by Amazon